THE ONLY EXCEPTION

www.abbiegracecreations.com

Ordering Information:

Quantity sales. Special discounts are available on quantity purchases by corporations, associations, and others. For details, contact the publisher at the address above.

Currently available on amazon.com.

Printed in the United States of America

First Edition

To the many people who have shown me that there is always an exception— Even to the idea that 15-year-old girls can't publish novels.

"The greater danger for most of us lies not in setting our mark too high and falling short, but in setting our aim too low and achieving our mark."

—Michelangelo

THE ONLY EXCEPTION

To Alexis ♡
You're exceptional!
Don't let anyone or
anything stand in your
way.
Love,
Abigail ♡

ONE

A high pitched shriek pierces the silence of the back hallway at Allerton High School. "Shhh! Amy! Shut up!" I whisper harshly. My voice reverberates vociferously off the blue and white walls. "You're going to get us thrown in detention on the last day of school! I have a flight to catch, remember?"

"How could I forget when you never shut up about it?" Amy retorts, momentarily lapsing out of her ecstatic state of cardiac arrest.

Allow me to introduce myself: Andrea Kailani Maverick. Seventeen, eleventh grade here at Allerton High, divorced parents from Hawaii, surfer/skateboarder/snowboarder (both competitively and for kicks). That about covers my life. Nothing quite so exciting as a romantic young girl getting swept off her feet by a handsome stranger or even a dog getting rabies, but that's life. I've never even had a pet, even though that's all I've ever asked for for birthdays and Christmases and Easters and all those other holidays.

Anyway, my friend here is currently suffering from an apparent heart attack behind the science labs. Oh, sheesh, it reeks back here. The freshmen must be dissecting fish in Biology. Lucky them. I hate the smell of formaldehyde.

The reason Amy is about to pass out is because the "love of her life" (or the past month, same difference) just texted her to ask her to come on a weekend long camping trip with his family. I can't help but laugh, because the last time Amy went camping, she ended up burning out the battery in our car because she couldn't live without air conditioning for more than two hours. Then again, she'd sooner bungee jump off the Empire State Building than turn down a date with Logan Cross.

"So, what do I say?" she asks despairingly, staring at me with her pleading blue eyes. Amy can manipulate her eyes more than anyone I've ever seen. She's made them striking and sharp before, but now, they've turned soft and innocent to coerce me into aiding her. I raise an eyebrow quizzically.

"You really expect me to know?" I question skeptically. "You didn't have a stroke or anything, did you?"

"I'm desperate here!" Her voice sounds as panicked as if she were about to be pushed off a cliff (or something to that effect). Oh, Amy. I love her, but she can be a bit of a drama queen sometimes.

"Well, you might want to check with your mom before running off into the woods with Logan," I point out.

"See? You're a genius," she replies, tapping out a text to her mother. I swear, that girl's thumbs are going to fall off her hands if she texts much faster.

"Alright, well, I've gotta get out of here. I have to turn in that last paper to Mr. Clarke before I can run off to catch my flight," I remind her, walking towards my advanced english class. Heels clicking on the tiled floor alert me to Amy's presence staying close behind me. The vibration of her cellphone when her mother responds even echoes back here.

"She said we have to talk about it when I get home," Amy updates me after a moment of the clack of her heels and the smack of my rubber slippers (or flip-flops as mainlanders call them here in New York. Flip-flops? Really? You couldn't have come up with a more creative name than that? I know, rubber slippers are "meh", but really?).

"Blah," I respond. "Text me after the talk to let me know the verdict."

"So, excited about Grammy and Papaw's?"

"More than you know," I reply truthfully. "A whole summer of sun, surf and no parents."

"And…"

"And my eighteenth birthday," I add with a nod. She grins as we make a sharp right into Mr. Clarke's classroom and she flips her blonde hair over her shoulder. "Mr. Clarke?" The balding, fifty-something man looks up from several papers with a red pen in his hand.

Mr. Clarke is by far my favorite teacher. He's witty, sarcastic and goes out of his way to help his students. It's not often you find a high school teacher willing to give you one on one help with a paper during lunch.

"Ah, Andrea, thank you," he says, extending his hand to take my paper. "I trust you missing our last class has to do with summer plans?"

"Hawaii to visit my grandparents," I reply, nodding. He smiles.

"Well, I suppose we shall see you next year?" he asks.

"Unless something drastic happens, I'll be back," I promise, grinning.

"Until then, Miss Maverick," he bids. I nod and head back out into the hall. Amy throws her arms around me in a brief hug and then pulls back, thrusting a dense package into my arms.

"I was going to tell you not open it until your birthday, but I want to watch you," she chatters eagerly. I smile and tear the paper off the rectangular parcel.

"Amy! You got me *This Present Darkness*?" I squeal. "Thank you!"

"It's the double volume," she adds. "With *Piercing the Darkness* too." I squeak again. I do that when I'm excited for some odd reason. An old habit I never grew out of, I guess.

"Thank you, thank you, thank you! I can read this on the plane!" I engulf her in a hug and, pulling back, slap her one more high five.

"Just do me two favors: call me if you meet any cute guys and hang loose out on those waves," she requests, flashing me the "hang loose" sign, also known as a shaka. I stick my tongue out and flash one right back at her, smiling. I've always thought it was ironic that a shaka sign is basically the sign for "play" in sign language, only rotated side to side instead of flicked downward, since telling a surfer to hang loose is like telling a kid to go play after opening presents on Christmas morning. She laughs and I turn away from the last look at my only New York friend I'm going to get for the next three months.

Outside in the parking lot, the backseat of my mother's pink Mary Kay Cadillac is stuffed with luggage. She got the car for being the top Mary Kay seller two years ago. I wonder if a car is enough to make up the fact that she ruined her family over it. Well, the job that gave it to her. I'm not saying my dad isn't to blame or anything, it's just— Oh, never mind. Parent-issue-free summer. Sun. Surf. Grammy and Papaw. Nothing will ruin my summer. (If this was a made-for-TV movie, this would be where my mom says "Sorry sweetheart, change of plans. The trip is off." Thank God my life is not a made-for-TV movie.)

I pop up the bubblegum-colored trunk lid and stuff my backpack in the compartment, happy to switch it for my favorite canvas hobo bag, which is all packed up for the plane ride from New York City, New York to Los Angelos, California, where I'll transfer to another flight to Oahu, Hawaii. I'll practically fly over my dad's house in South San Francisco.

If I weren't going to the famous North Shore of Oahu, I would be disappointed I'm not staying with my dad. It's just thirty-one minutes away from Mavericks (a super amazing world famous surf spot, in addition to my last name). I get to drive out to the spot as often as I can and watch some of the best surfers alive take on the monster waves. As often as I can, though, usually means about five times all summer, due to daddy-daughter time or daddy-daughter time gone wrong thanks to my dad's company and all it's stupid meetings.

"Of course. Of course, Bella! We need our ladies to look their best!" my mother gushes into a bluetooth earpiece. Her phone is in her hand and her fingers rapidly tap out an email to one customer or another. "Alright. I will have your shipment to you as soon as I get the list. Okay. Ciao!" She taps the earpiece and cuts the call. She doesn't look up as she finishes her email and I slide into the passenger seat. "Hello sweetheart, how was school?"

"Fantastic as always," I quip sarcastically. "Amy gave me that Frank Perretti book I was wanting as an early birthday present, and the sequel, too."

"Well, that was sweet of her," she replies. "All ready for your flight?"

"Yeah," I say, itching to finish rereading *Three Hours Too Soon* by Adam Reed so I can begin *This Present Darkness*. "I'll miss you though."

"Aw, I'll miss you too, honey," she says absently, touching her earpiece and answering another call. I sigh and reach for my novel. *Three Hours Too Soon* is about a terminally ill girl named Jane and her friendship with a boy named Lucas Blake. It's dreadfully tragic, yet such a good story that I want to read it again and again.

Still talking, my mother bats away the book and gives me what my father would call her Disney Villain Evil Eye. It's that look that Disney villains get when they're about to go bezerk, like before Maleficent turns into the dragon or the evil queen gives Snow White the apple. She probably thinks her phone call is going to end in time to have a conversation with me for more than five minutes. I roll my eyes and turn on the radio instead, which she promptly turns down and goes back to her conversation.

Some people pity me. Whenever I say "my parents are divorced," the only people that get it are the other kids with separated or divorced parents. Everyone else looks at me like I'm a lost kitten or something, and for me, even some of the kids with broken families don't get it. I get it that my parents don't love each other anymore. No, the part that I hate about all this is that my parents are workaholic divorced parents who could care less about my existence most of the time and when they do care about my existence, they care too much.

I think I might be the only teenage girl in the world who's not happy about getting entire designer clothing lines and a new Macbook or iPad for every other holiday. It's like they compete with each other. Like, if I like one parent's presents better than the other's, I love that parent more than the other. Like I said before, all I ever wanted was a puppy.

Quick explanation of my parents' abundant wealth: My dad started some business when he was twenty-two and my mother became a Mary Kay consultant around that time. Then, my mom had me, worked her tail off to be a good Mary Kay seller and a good mom, got a ton of promotions and suddenly Mary Kay was a higher priority than little me, practically living at my grandparents' house. My dad's company took off and is now one of the biggest names in business in a bazillion countries.

Fast-forward to after the divorce and my father has been named every other magazine's Businessman of the Year or whatever title they can give him, made a ton of money (like, in the seven figures a year for going on six years) and my mother is one of the top two Mary Kay Cosmetic sellers (Not to mention they've ruined their marriage and all that, but you know, "details, details, darlings" as my mother's fashion designer friends would say). Since she became known in the Mary Kay world as "Charlotte Maverick," she kept the name.

About twenty minutes later, we pull up in front of John F. Kennedy airport. My mother's conversation is finally over and she hops out of the car, her heels clicking neatly on the blacktop. Often, I have moments when I just can't believe the casual woman in my baby photos is the same woman I see before my eyes. This is definitely one of those moments. 42 years old with not a grey hair in sight, always made over, never a hair out of place. Today, she's dressed in a chic black pencil skirt, an off-white ruffly blouse and a pair of red, pointed toe Christian Louboutin pumps. A string of pearls hangs around her neck, matching the pearl and gold teardrop earrings just above it. Her perfectly manicured hand opens the back door and pulls out my entire set of matching rainbow striped Jenni Chan luggage. She bought it for me just after the divorce when my father decided to move to California. Before the divorce, my parents and I lived in a house near my grandparents on Oahu. I was thirteen when my mom and I moved.

Even though moving away from Dad and my favorite place in the world was hard, Amy made it a little easier. We wore the exact same *Peter Pan* t-shirt, similar colored skinny jeans, and black Converse on the first day of school and got paired up as lab partners. We've been practically inseparable ever since, even though our outfits and some of our movie taste were where the similarities ended. Amy has an older brother in college and two younger brothers. Her parents have been happily married for 25+ years. Amy is also a believer in all those common lies about love. True love, happily ever after, love at first sight, all that stuff. She's also suffering from a disease that's known commonly as CBCS (Cute Boy Craziness Syndrome).

Do I believe in that stuff? Short answer: no. Long answer: N-O. No. Have you been paying attention? My parents fell in love, got married and had me. For about the first eight years of my life, it seemed like they loved each other. I mean, they fought, but who doesn't fight? Then, about after the time I turned nine, the fights started escalating. No longer simply heated conversations, but screaming, insulting and bringing up everything including the kitchen sink. They started over the littlest things, too. For four years, they tried to patch things up, but it just got worse. They tried counseling, they tried a "mommy/daddy vacation" for two weeks in the Bahamas, they tried living separately for a little and then getting back together, they tried everything. Eventually, they just went down to the courthouse and signed the papers. My point is that between seeing my parents' relationship fall apart and seeing Amy or my friends in Hawaii break their hearts time and time again, I've discovered that even the strongest of bonds break. I don't want that. Fine with me if someone else wants to take that risk, but I don't. I don't ever want to do to a child what my parents have done to me. I don't want to do to a man what my mother has done to my father. I don't want what happened to my mother to happen to me.

My mother takes two of the suitcases by the handles and rolls them in to the airport, with me trailing behind her, towing another suitcase. She checks them at the desk, checking me in for my flight simultaneously. I carry my purse and my black Nike duffel bag over my shoulder and watch people mill around in the lobby. Families greeting kids home from college, a husband returning home from a trip to his wife and daughter, a few people obviously going on business trips and several families prepped and ready for the same thing I am: Summer vacation.

"Alright, tell Grammy and Papaw I said hi," my mother reminds me. "And call me when you get to L.A. And when you arrive on Oahu. And if anything happens."

"Okay, Mom," I reply. "See you in September."

"Be careful with your knee," she warns. "Remember what Maria told you during therapy. Use your tape if you need, wear the brace if it's tired, and don't get in trouble."

I have chondromalacia (also known as runner's knee) in my left knee, and have for a long time. Basically, chondromalacia is when the cartilage at the bottom of your kneecap softens or deteriorates. When that happens, your knee slides around in the joint to sides or angles it's not supposed to. Wearing a brace that holds your kneecap in place helps a lot of people, which I do sometimes, but it's never been bad enough to need surgery. Corrective surgeries exist, but physical therapy works well enough for me. I wear a heavy-duty brace during snowboard and skateboarding competitions and training as extra reassurance, but I can't wear one in the water. Instead, I just use a water-resistant tape that pulls the muscles into position, which relieves some tension in my leg.

"I won't, Mom. I'm not going to do anything stupid."

"I love you, sweetheart," she croons. She pulls me in for a hug and I echo her words.

"I love you too, Mom." At that, I tote my duffel bag and gigantic purse back to security, thinking only of the summer ahead of me. With my shorts, teal rubber slippers and bright green "GEEK" sleeveless tee, I'm ready. Come at me, summer.

Once through security, I walk past all the little shops, restaurants and gates, coming to my own gate soon enough. I pass a Starbucks and a Panda Express, both of which I strongly consider buying something from, but decide against it when I glance at the clock. Not bad. Half an hour to spare. I sit down at the gate and pull my book out, wondering when Amy's going to text me. Only thirty pages left, if that. Oh, wait. If my calculations are correct, the last thirty pages of the book are the also the saddest pages of the book. Great, I'm going to be sobbing like a crazy person in the middle of this airport terminal. Oh, well. Who cares if they think I'm insane?

So, of course, I sit here in my blue leather airport chair for the next twenty minutes, alternating between reading, trying to find a comfortable spot in these stupid chairs, crying and dreaming about the movie that comes out in a week until the gate agents call the economy plus passengers.

Ever since I had this big fight with both of my parents about flying first class every time I fly, they've put me in economy plus, which is about six inches more leg room than coach, but essentially the same thing. It's the closest they can get to first class without me blowing up. Even so, sometimes, they still spring for first class around holidays, saying it's "for a special occasion." NEWS FLASH: It's not special if it happens every other time I fly somewhere.

"Boarding pass?" the gate agent asks, extending her hand. I hand it over and she scans it. "Enjoy your flight, Miss Maverick."

"Thanks," I reply, following the elderly couple in front of me through the line.

I board the plane and find my seat fairly quickly. As soon as I stow my Nike bag in the overhead bin, I situate myself in my seat, pull out *This Present Darkness* (having finished *Three Hours Too Soon*) and my glasses and await a text from Amy. Sure enough, as some business woman sits down and gets comfortable in the seat next to me, my iPhone buzzes. "SHE SAID YES!!!!!!!!!!!!!!!!" it reads. A second later, it buzzes again in my hand. "IM GOING CAMPING WITH LOGAN AND HIS FAMILY AND HIS MOM SAID SHES REALLY GLAD IM COMING AND YEAH IM FREAKING OUT."

"YAY!" I text back. "Have fun with Logan! On the plane to Oahu right now." I tag a little smiley face on the end of the message.

"Once again rubbing it in my face I'm not going to Hawaii," she responds with a little emoticon, who's sticking his tongue out at me. "Love you girl! Have fun!"

"Thanks! You too!" I put my phone on airplane mode and dive into my book.

TWO

Twelve hours and one flight transfer later, I'm walking off the plane in what would be sunny Oahu, if it wasn't ten o'clock at night. Even so, I can see that the stars are bright and the sky is clear through the gigantic terminal window as I make my way to the baggage claim. I manage to dig my phone out of the depths of my purse, punch in my mom's number and listen to it ring. "You've reached Charlotte

Maverick. Please leave me a message with your name and phone number and I'll get back to you as soon as I can. Thank you."

"Hi Mom, it's me. I'm in Oahu right now. No one kidnapped me, my flight didn't crash and I'm okay. Love you." I hang up, wondering if she'll call me back just to say hi. Doubtful. Very doubtful.

Regardless of the time, my grandparents wait for me at the baggage claim looking more awake than if it was the middle of the day.

"Annie!" Grammy exclaims, smiling and holding out her arms. I grin and set down my bags to envelope her in a hug. Her familiar scent of perfume and baking ingredients puts me at ease instantly. "My goodness, you're so tall! I don't know whether you grew or if I just forgot what it's like being face to face with my girl. It feels like forever since we last saw you!"

"I know, I missed you," I reply, hugging Papaw, who smells of motor oil. Suffice it to say, he's not as active in the kitchen as my grandmother. He's a motorcycle guy.

"Amped for some surfing, Kiddo?" he asks, a gleam in his eye.

"You bet," I laugh. My bright patterned luggage comes around the carousel and Papaw pulls it off for me.

"Gosh, you'd think she was staying for the whole summer, wouldn't you?" he teases. Grammy laughs.

"I sure hope so," she replies. The three of us head outside, hop in their car (a beat up, old minivan) and head off to their house.

Of all the places in the world, this one is the place that feels most like home to me. I like New York and I like California, but Oahu is just Oahu. There's no place like it. And there's no place like my grandparents' house, either. 72 Alapio Rd. Big, but not huge. Modern, but not cold. Cozy, but stylish. When I was seven, my grandparents let me decorate one of the guest rooms as my own since I was already practically living there. I redecorated it about 3 years ago to what it is now.

I pass through the aqua and white entryway, living room and kitchen and head down the hall to the second door on the left. My small surfboard door sign still hangs at eye level with "Andrea Kalani" painted in delicate white lettering. As I push open the white door, the first thing my eyes travel to is the poster for *Chasing Mavericks* and my signed Bethany Hamilton poster. She was in San Fransisco to speak at a convention and my dad let me go for a day. It was great. She's an awesome girl and a terrific surfer to top it all off.

My ukelele stands on my dresser, across from my bed. Dropping my bags, I hurl myself onto my *Endless Summer* graphic duvet and flop back, sighing. It's good to be home.

In the corner stands my favorite guitar I had my dad send here. My mom's brother that lives in Tennessee taught me to play when I was little, and I've never really quit playing. It's easy to lose myself in someone else's life when I'm reading, but it makes my own life better when I play music.

Speaking of music, I extract my phone from my purse and hit "Shuffle" on my songs. It lands on "The Reckless and the Brave" by All Time Low and I plug it into my speaker set on my nightstand. I start to unpack my many suitcases, so it can really feel like I'm home, as I sing along. I don't know why my mother insisted I bring things like dresses and high heels to a place where I'm going to be in the ocean all day. Maybe it's me, but I don't even really get that whole concept. You know, like, you wear a fancy and probably uncomfortable dress to Prom to dance and have fun, but you wouldn't wear a fancy dress to bed or when you're just going to sit on the couch and relax. Same thing with sweatpants. You wouldn't wear sweatpants to Prom even though they'd be ten times more comfortable than the dress, but you would wear them to the grocery. I just don't understand. And I'm a bit of a sweatpants enthusiast.

The many fashion shows my mother drags me to are a different matter entirely, due to the fact that that kind of fashion is art that skeletons walk down a runway in. No one else on the face of the planet could physically wear almost anything I've seen during any fashion week ever anywhere but to walk down a runway, and even that would take some intense training. Why? Just why? Why would anyone want to wear a giant strapless dress that looks like someone just knotted a bunch of tulle together and added four bazillion layers of the stuff to the skirt to make it poofy and essentially walk on stilts? I just don't get it.

"Annie! Weather's on!" my grandfather calls. I run out to the living room, pausing the music and leaving my unpacking and thoughts about fashion behind, and jump over the back of the couch, legs outstretched. Yes, I watch the weather. That's one of the unique things about Hawaii. The weather is never just the boring old weather channel. The weather is the surf conditions for the upcoming days, thus bringing with it a tide of excitement because, surfing (duh). "So what do you think? Need a couple of days to get back in the swing of things or ready to get back in the pocket tomorrow?" Papaw jokes.

"You kidding? We may not have waves up north, but I can hold my own on a skateboard," I boast with a playfully cocky smile. "Didn't think I would stop training, did you?"

"A true Maverick," my Grammy calls from the kitchen. "Wild and free."

"And of the sea," Papaw adds, smiling warmly. My grandpa picked the name Kailani for my middle name because it means "of the sea." He was the one who taught me to surf. A long time ago, my dad used to surf, too. He enjoyed it a lot, but decided his company was more important. Add it to the list.

"Alright, we can check the conditions for Sunset and Waimea. Let's wait a few weeks until we head to Banzai," Papaw plans. I nod, thinking of the nasty cut I got two years ago on the coral reef at Banzai Pipeline. Great surf spot for people who know what they're doing, but there's a coral reef just a short distance under the surface that makes it a hundred times more dangerous. "Oh, that reminds me. There's a couple of competitions coming up that signups close for this week. We can go get you signed up tomorrow if you want."

"Yes!" I determine quickly. "Yes. Absolutely. How's McKayla?" McKayla is my preschool best friend that I grew up surfing with. I see her every time I come for holidays, and we always make it a point to go surfing together like old times. We still text back and forth when I'm in New York, but it's just not the same.

"Good, last time I saw her," Grammy assures. "She's got a boyfriend now. Michael, the boy you two used to play with all the time when you were little."

"Michael Chase?" I ask. "He's not bad."

"He's quite a nice boy," she agrees, nodding.

"There's also a family that moved here from Australia about a year and a half ago," Papaw updates me. "The dad's a board maker and owns a surf shop. All handmade boards, no pop-outs. His two older boys work in the shop with him and his wife. One of the boys is your age and the other is in college. There's a younger girl, too."

"Great," I reply, not really paying attention. I'm watching the flashing lights on the TV screen around Waimea Bay. Good. Not the winter swells, but not quite the summer calm either. Decently sized waves to get me back in the swing of things. By the way, pop-outs are mass-produced, machine made boards that are generally not as good as a handmade board. I have a board that was made by a huge company, but it's not considered a pop-out because it's handmade. I yawn. "Well, if I'm getting up and getting back into the island schedule, I better get to sleep. Wake me up when you're ready to go."

Papaw kisses my forehead and Grammy pecks my cheek on my way out of the room. I finish emptying all of my suitcases into the closet and dresser and switch my denim shorts for flannel PJ ones. After brushing my teeth and weaving my hair back into a french braid, I burrow down into the covers and glance at my bright green surfboard in the corner, before drifting off to sleep.

THREE

The next morning, I wake up from the most amazing dream. I was back in Oahu for the whole summer and— wait. Slowly, my eyelids flutter open. It wasn't a dream. I'm really home for the whole summer.

I hear several knocks on my bedroom door and Papaw pokes his head in the door. I yawn and stretch, hopping out of bed and rushing to get my things together. "Ready to go?" he inquires.

"Almost. Let me get my suit on and I'll be ready," I reply. He heads back into the living room and I quickly change into my favorite plain black bikini, accompanied by my short sleeved green rash guard shirt. Throw on a pair of cotton shorts and I'm ready to go.

For swimming, I'd wear a tankini or a one-piece suit, but since I wear a rash guard, it's easier to wear a bikini. If I don't, the fabric bunches up under my shirt. The rash guard is to prevent chafing from the sand or wax on the board and irritation from the water. They're also used in competition to identify one surfer from another in the water, kind of like jerseys. Competition rash guards each have a number on them and usually come in five colors, as the rounds of a competition have four or five surfers a heat typically.

"Have fun, Kiddo!" my Grammy calls as I dash past her.

"Love you! See you later!" I yell, running out the door with my surfboard in tow. Papaw straps it to the top of the van and I hop in the passenger seat.

"Somebody going surfing?" a familiar voice calls. I turn to see my childhood best friend, McKayla, jogging across the street with her own bright purple board under her arm. "Mind if I hitch a ride?"

"Mac!" I exclaim. "Come on, we're headed to Waimea."

"Aw, no Pipeline?" she jokes. "Somebody's going soft! Not becoming a shubie, are you?"

"No, you kook," I tease. Shubies are people that dress and talk like surfers, but can't actually ride and kooks are beginners that only surf to try to look cool. They're not popular in the surfing community. Papaw straps her board on top of mine as McKayla clambers in next to me. "If anybody's going soft, it's the girl who didn't think I could surf Mavericks!"

"Hey, you can't blame me for wanting you to come back alive! It's basically you and Laird Hamilton that are crazy enough to surf those waves," she fires back.

In addition to watching the pros surf it, I may have surfed Mavericks. Just once. Or twice. Even though the waves didn't kill me, my mother almost did when she saw the videos, but it was worth it. Definitely the ride of the lifetime. Gliding down the face of a monster wave with nothing but a leash on your ankle tying you down. "Did you just put me in the same category of surfers as Laird Hamilton?"

"Don't get a big head just yet," she reprimands, twisting her long black hair into a bun. "You can do that after you win the Pro Curl if you would ACTUALLY COME IN THE WINTER!" She exclaims the last part loudly, being less than subtle about her wishes.

"I know, I know, I've tried," I answer as Papaw pulls out of the driveway. "My parents would never let me. Not for that long."

"You do remember you're turning 18 at the end of the summer, right?" she suggests. "You know, legal adult, you'll be able to vote and not to mention, buy your own house."

"Yeah, uh, how?" I ask, french braiding my brown locks. "My parents would disown me."

"Win the Pro Curl, get fifty thousand dollars in prize money, get some sponsors and live the dream!" she shouts.

"Oh, of course, I forgot," I reply sarcastically. "Silly me."

"Before you two take on the Pro Curl, you'd better start training for those local competitions," Papaw points out, throwing the beater into park. McKayla and I hop out onto the patch of grass we parked on and start unstrapping our boards. I glance at the waves. Good size, nice pace and there's almost no one out there. "Pick you up for lunch?"

"Nah, we'll walk down to Tara's, then walk back from there," I reply. He nods.

"Okay, see you groms later," he calls, pulling out. Groms are what little kid surfers are called.

"Later, grey belly!" I shout back, calling my grandpa the surfer slang for old guy. McKayla glances at me with an evil glint in her eye.

"Race ya!" she shouts suddenly, dashing to the sand. I run after her, my long legs quickly outrunning her shorter ones.

"What was that you were saying about going soft, Gidget?" I shout. Gidget = girl midget. Surfer lingo for short girl surfer. At 5' 9", I'm not exactly a Gidget. She laughs.

"Okay, point taken," she pants. Moments later, we're paddling out to the lineup (just behind where the waves start to break) and battling it out to catch the first wave. In the end, I win, dropping in on my first wave in what feels like forever. I love this feeling. It always feels like flying, no matter how old I get or how many times I've done it.

Like it's nothing, I swerve my board to snap the lip of the wave, which is basically doing a sharp turn that causes a shower of sea water to spray up behind me. "And she's still got it!" McKayla yells as I do a couple more tricks.

"Now let's see you, paddlepuss!" I call back as I paddle back towards her. She goes after a wave and passes me on my way back out. On my next wave, I start playing with some of my favorite skateboarding tricks, adapting them just a bit for the water.

"What was that?!" she yells as I swim towards her.

"A skateboarding trick," I answer.

"Maybe I should get into skateboarding." I paddle up next to her and lay out on my board, my stomach against the deck of the board.

"Maybe you should," I suggest. "It's good for coming up with tricks. Although, it's not so good for keeping your bones all together."

"Ever broken anything?" she asks, taking a cue from me and laying back on her board.

"Nope. I've seen kids fall at the skate park before though and there were one or two that were particularly nasty," I reply.

"Like, how particularly?"

"Like, bone sticking out," I respond nonchalantly.

"Yeah, that's a little… gnarly…"

"Yeah, but only a few people have that happen, and that's when they're doing what's called extreme stupid," I point out. "Or they're just barneys." Barneys are the same thing as kooks (not big purple dinosaurs that sing "I Love You"). Don't worry, I'm used to explaining this stuff. You have no idea how long it took me not to say the surfer slang for everything in school in New York. My classmates used to stare at me like I had turned green or something. "So, moving on. New around the island?"

"Well… Michael may have asked me out," she admits. She smiles widely, unable to contain her grin.

"That's awesome," I reply, smiling back. "You've known him for practically forever."

"So you're not mad?" she clarifies.

"Mac, just because I don't think true love exists doesn't mean I can't be happy for you," I assure her. "No matter your decisions, I'll stand by you. But some decisions, we'll be having a serious talk about."

"Don't worry," she laughs.

"Good," I return. "Seriously, though, be careful, okay?" She nods. I notice a surfer about twenty yards or so away. Pretty tall guy, decently skilled. After further observation, I notice he's doing skateboarding tricks, like I was a minute ago. Choka, dude. I turn my attention back to McKayla. "What else is new?"

"Um, about a year and a half ago this Australian guy, Mr. Hensley came over and started a business and bought a house and all that," she updates me. "Then halfway through the school year, his kids and wife came over too. There's a boy that's twenty, I think, Daniel, a boy our age, Sawyer, and a girl that's about in 6th grade, Julia. They all surf and they're all great. Sawyer's about the most fun person you'll ever meet. Smart, not exactly ugly, and, well, Aussie." She pronounces "Aussie" like "Ozzie" that way Australians do, to which I laugh.

"Sounds like quite the superman," I reply, glancing back over at the other surfer. He's gotten a bit closer. Just so long as he knows his wave etiquette, as my grandma calls it. Surfing is a bit like driving. Just like a driver has the right-of-way in certain scenarios on the road, a surfer has the right-of-way on certain waves. No one likes a drop in.

"He's not as good as Mikey, but he's nice," McKayla agrees. "He had us rolling on the floor at youth group with some of his stories, though. He tells us what he does and what the Australian stereotype would be for stuff, and I don't believe a word of it, but it's hilarious."

A sick wave starts building behind us and I sit up, lean forward and start paddling. Zoning in, I drop into the wave and push myself up on my hands, about to pop up, when out of nowhere, someone cuts in front of me and what I think is a foot hits me in the right eye. I lose my balance and roll off my board, getting dragged under and knocked around in the swirling water as the wave passes over me like the spin cycle of a washing machine. The leash of my board tugs on my ankle and my lungs scream for air. My vision starts to go fuzzy and I'm seeing colorful spots.

Somewhere in the confusion, my head comes up and I start gagging. My board pops up next to me and I grab on. My head is throbbing. I don't think I can open my eye. Whether I can or not, it hurts. The other eye, though full of saltwater, can see just fine. I know, because I can see a figure about fifty yards towards shore, paddling back in my direction.

"Annie! Are you okay?!" Mac calls, paddling up beside me. It's probably a good thing my ability to speak has been neutralized, otherwise I'd be spewing as much profanity as I am water.

"WHAT in the HECK was that supposed to be?!" I cough/shout towards the other surfer. I wretch and hack a few more times and climb up on my board, closing my non-injured eye to keep the bright sunlight out. "No snaking, barney! If you learned yesterday, pick a different spot to surf!"

"Hey, woah," an unfamiliar voice replies. "I didn't mean to hit you! And I'm not exactly a barney. What did I do that was so wrong?"

"Oh, nothing, except you dropped in on my wave, kicked me in the eye and caused me to almost drown," I reply tartly.

"Oh, yeah, I caused you to almost drown," the voice scoffs. "Let's not forget that you weren't looking where you were going in the least. I'm not entirely to blame." Wow, talk about nerve! I don't even have a face to match the voice yet and I already don't like whoever's voice it is. It sounds like a teenage boy's voice that's deep, but young and has a foreign accent that I cannot place in the middle of my jumbled, under oxygenated thoughts. He sighs and says, much more calmly, "Here, let me see your eye." Slowly, I peel my fingers off of my right eye. Reluctantly and painfully, I open both of my eyes, waiting for the receptors to adjust.

As I become accustomed to the light, a pair of deep blue eyes stare into mine worriedly. A boy about my age sits on his surfboard, dressed in light blue board shorts and a white rash guard. His wet brown hair is finger-combed in a swoop off to his left so as to stay out of his eyes. "Oh, gosh, that's gonna be a shiner. It's already swollen a bit, but that'll be black by tomorrow."

"Great. First day back and I'm already banged up," I sigh.

"Well, Mac, you staying out or coming back with me?"

"What do you think, gremmie?" she asks. Gremmie is another word for inexperienced or young surfer. "By the way, nice to see you, Sawyer." She takes off, paddling into a wave to ride in to shore.

"I'm really, really sorry. My name's Sawyer. Is there anything I can do to make it up to you?" he asks. It's only then that I manage to put two and two together. His accent is Australian, watered down a bit with some American pronunciation, but none the less Aussie. This must be the kid Mac was raving about a minute ago.

"Just don't cut me off on this next wave," I request cooly, paddling into the wave. The ride is smooth, so I do a couple of snaps, just to make sure it doesn't go completely to waste and to blow off some steam. I meet McKayla on the beach, talking to an older boy that looks similar to Sawyer, but with hair that's darker than his brother's.

"Nice going, Sawyer," the boy yells in Sawyer's direction, with a thicker version of his accent and not as deep of a voice. "My clueless brother clocked you in the face?"

"Yeah, pretty much," I call back, throwing my board down in the sand and running one hand over my salty, drenched, braided hair.

"I'm Daniel," he introduces, extending his hand to me. I take it and shake it.

"Andrea," I reply. Sawyer has caught up and drops his board next to mine.

"Do you guys have a ride?" Daniel inquires. McKayla shakes her head. I, meanwhile, have a headache the size of Texas and just watching her shake her head makes mine hurt. My jaw doesn't feel to good, either. This kid has some leg strength, man. I'd expect nothing less from a surfer, but I'd be lying if I said I guessed anything even close to getting kicked in the face by a fellow surfer to happen anytime soon. "I've got my car with me if you want one."

"We were going to walk down to Tara's at lunchtime, but obviously, that's not happening," McKayla fills them in. "Annie? What do you want to do?"

"I don't care," I reply, just trying to get away from this idiot as soon as possible.

"I've had plenty of black eyes in my life," Daniel says. "Head's probably pounding right about now, right?" I nod slightly. "Yeah, we'll get you home. Sawyer, get the boards. Mac, do you want to get her situated?"

"I'm fine," I lie, not wanting to seem wimpy. "I'll be okay." Sawyer picks up both his and my board and straps them to the back of Daniel's navy blue, open top Jeep, pausing to open my door for me. I slide in and lean my head back against the headrest, hoping for relief that doesn't come. The other three climb in and Daniel talks directions with McKayla. I try to alleviate some of the pressure and ease the pain in my head, but it doesn't help much. Fantastic. Simply fantastic.

FOUR

The ride is only five minutes, but still painful, since my head feels like it's being whacked with a baseball bat every time we drive over a little bump. Upon arrival, I again decline help as I climb out of the car. I push open the front door and kick off my rubber slippers. "Grammy! We're back!" I call, almost wincing at the shot of pain through my head.

"Hi sweetheart, I though you and McKayla wer-" Grammy cuts off her own sentence as she emerges from the kitchen and lays eyes on me. "Annie, what happened to your eye?"

"Nice to know it looks good already," I grumble. "This genius decided to drop in on my wave and kicked me in the eye when he cut me off."

"I'm really sorry, Mrs. Maverick," Sawyer apologizes. "I really didn't mean to. I just got too close, didn't see her and I couldn't stop."

"Oh, no worries," she assures him. "Annie, it really doesn't look that bad. It'll heal up in a few days." No worries, my eye. Literally. You want to tell me I have no worries, take a look at my face. "We'll just get some ice for that. You go lay down on the couch, Annie. McKayla, could you go back and get one or two pillows off her bed?" McKayla nods and disappears down the hall. "Sawyer, Daniel, make yourselves at home," Grammy invites. "You can put on a movie if you like. Help yourself to anything that's not covered in tin foil in the fridge."

"Thanks. I'll go get her board," Daniel says, exiting the entry hall. An awkward silence fills the room, feeling louder than any sort of noise.

"Want to watch something?" Sawyer asks a moment later. I shrug and point at the DVD cabinet.

"Help yourself," I reply. He strides across the room, opening the glass door to examine my grandparents' DVD collection. Eventually, he holds up *The Avengers*. I shrug again as I lie down on the long, leather sectional couch, back turned to both screen and idiot.

Sawyer occupies one of the other sides of the sectional and McKayla emerges, carrying my favorite pillow. Regardless of the fancy sheets I have at my parents' houses, this is by far my favorite pillowcase ever. It's white, with big splotches of pink dye here and there. On each splotch is a small gathering of three or four butterflies, with other tiny color spots scattered around them of teal and yellow. The texture is silk-like, but not in the least bit stiff or cold.

I try to get comfortable, but even after applying the squishy reusable ice pack Grammy gives me wrapped in a towel, I'm still shifting and squirming, switching back and forth from laying on either side to my back. "Do you want some help?" Sawyer offers. I feel like being stubborn, but the discomfort gets the better of me.

"If you don't mind," I reply meekly. He stands and crosses to me.

"Sit up for a second," he instructs. I sit up and move the pillow out of the way. He takes it from my hands and arranges it along with a couch pillow to support my head a little bit more. McKayla returns from my room with a scarf and Sawyer ties the ice pack around my face like a blindfold, then returns to his seat. I lay back down, close my other eye and try to relax. The cold seeps through the scarf and slowly numbs the upper right corner of my face. I hear the door shut and someone that's most likely Daniel plop down in the spot next to Sawyer, when suddenly, music starts playing from the dining room table.

McKayla hops up and brings my phone over to me. Without taking off my blindfold/ice pack, I answer it. "Hello?"

"Hey, surfer girl," my dad greets cheerfully. "How's Oahu?"

"It's good," I say, only half lying. "How's Cali?"

"Oh, the usual," he replies nonchalantly. "Grammy & Papaw?"

"Terrific," I assure. "Waves are good. You should've seen me this morning, I was charging on three or four of the waves I caught." Charging= on fire. Doing well. Tearing it up.

"Choka!" he laughs, meaning "awesome," basically. "I've gotta go. I just called to make sure you were okay. My next client just got here."

"Okay," I reply. "Love you. Bye, Dad."

"Love you too. Bye, Annie." The line goes dead.

I hang up and listen to *The Avengers* on the television for a bit, but the blissful quiet is quickly interrupted again. "Hello?"

"Hi honey, Grammy and Papaw said you went surfing earlier so I decided I'd try you again," my mother chatters away. "You're okay, right?"

"Yes, Mom, I'm fine," I fib.

"Okay sweetheart," she responds. "I've got another call coming and I've just arrived at a client's house. Call you later!"

"Sure, Mom," I promise. "Love you."

"Love you too," she echoes. "Bye."

"Bye." Another dead line. As Robert Downey Jr. talking through the television is the only sound in the room, my headache starts to settle back into a dull ache instead of a piercing throb.

I pull off my blindfold to set my phone on the coffee table in front of me and before I can close my eyes again, Sawyer looks at me curiously. "What?"

"You didn't tell them I kicked you in the face," he says confusedly. I close my eyes and sigh, tying the ice pack back around my face.

"I didn't want them to worry," I reply simply. That's only sort of the truth. If they heard I had a black eye, my mother would order me forty different kinds of coverup and about fifty different kinds of eye makeup. My dad would most likely want to get me some kind of gadget to hold an ice pack on my eye for me or a robot to do stuff for me. Seriously, when I get hurt, sometimes I just want a dad who will say "walk it off, you're fine" and a mom who will give me some Tylenol and tell me to sleep, not everything else I could possibly buy.

We sit like we are for about two more hours, with Grammy bringing sandwiches in at lunchtime and various movie watchers helping me take the ice pack off and tie it back on at 10-minute intervals. I notice Sawyer's hair, now dry, is a medium brown, almost like a cross between auburn and chocolate, that he runs his fingers through, sweeping it off to his left.

Grammy comes over a little later and evaluates my face. The swelling in my eye, according to her, has gone down, but the bruise will last about a week, maybe longer. Daniel and Sawyer get ready to leave after Grammy suggests I go lay down in my room for a little while.

"Sorry again," Sawyer apologizes on his way out the door.

"It's okay," I reply hesitantly, holding up a hand on my way back to my room.

"Later," they chorus in their Aussie accents. I carry my pillow back to my space and flop as gently as one can flop onto my sunset duvet.

"Thank you, Grammy," I say to no one in particular, grateful my grandmother could tell I needed to be rid of them. Sawyer, specifically. McKayla drops onto the giant bean bag in the corner. "Yeah, he's definitely the most fun person I've ever met. Likes to dance."

"Aw, come on, he's not that bad," she chides, trying not to laugh.

"Not that bad?! He kicked me in the face, Mac! Then, and this is the best part, he tried to act like it was *my* fault I almost drowned! What would you think if a guy cut you off on the road and totaled your car?" I ask, bringing memories of remarks shouted at other drivers and an ear-splitting car horn. "I've seen your road rage, Mac. That guy would be #1 on the CIA's 'wanted' list if you could make it happen."

McKayla can't hold it in any longer. Her light, loud laugh bursts forth and she just keeps laughing, unable to stop. "It's good to have you back," she laughs.

"Even when I'm all bruised up?"

"Definitely," she reassures, still giggling.

"Anyway, I just don't like him," I continue. "There's just bad news written all over the whole thing. Not to mention his stupid ego."

"Fine. Be that way. Just so long as you don't mind competing against him," she adds.

"Oh, I don't mind. I'll kick his butt any day," I respond. "Just like yours." She laughs again and chucks a teddy bear at me. "Foul! Attacking a maimed opponent! Disqualified!" I shout, throwing a pillow at her. She and I start throwing anything relatively soft we can find at each other, both of us shrieking with laughter. My door opens to reveal Papaw, who charges through the room with my surfboard in front of him as a shield.

"Cease and desist!" he commands. We do as he says, still giggling, and he sets my board in the corner. "Annie, if you're up for it, I can drive you to the offices for signups for those competitions I mentioned."

"Of course I'm up for it!" I reply enthusiastically. "What competitions?"

"The Oahu Juniors Championships, the Annual Pipeline and, maybe, just maybe, if you do well in the other competitions, regionals," he says.

"Seriously?!" I exclaim. "Thank you, thank you, thank you! But what if I make it past regionals? I'd qualify for state, right?"

"Right. After state, would possibly be nationals, and certain positions at nationals can get you a spot on the international team for the World Championships," he explains. "But that means you could be in this for the long haul. And a spot on the world champs team is extremely iffy."

"What about my parents? Did they agree to this?" I question. He shakes his head.

"I don't know. I haven't talked to them yet," he says. "I didn't know if you'd want me to."

"Why don't we wait and see about the first two, then figure out regionals after," I decide. He nods approvingly.

"Alright," he agrees. I shoot a glance at Mac.

"You want to come help sign me up?" I inquire. She shrugs.

"Got nothing better to do," she replies, standing. We follow Papaw out to the living room and slide on our rubber slippers, bidding goodbye to Grammy. I put on my dark shades, thankful for once that my mother bought the big ones that look like the kind celebrities wear in paparazzi photos. They're big enough to cover my eye and the discoloration spreading around it.

"Try not to get kicked in the eye this time," Grammy calls on my way out the door. I laugh loudly.

"Don't worry!" I answer. "We're only going to the surf offices. We'll be back soon."

The old beater clunks along, getting us from point A to point B in about fifteen minutes. A little bell rings as we open the glass door to the office. The white walls are covered in posters of great surfers like Kelly Slater and Laird Hamilton. A short girl's blonde ponytail evilly flips around as her head turns towards us from behind the front desk. "Mr. Maverick," Sally Emerson greets in her high-pitched voice, smiling. She looks to me with her smile becoming sweeter than a spoonful of sugar. "Annie! You're back!"

"Hi Sally." I reply through gritted teeth, grimacing as I take my glasses off. Her mouth drops open slightly, quirked up at the corners.

"What happened to you?" she asks in awe. I really need to look in the mirror. You'd think this would've occurred to me before we left the house.

"Sawyer Hensley," I reply.

"Really?" she asks, intrigued, knitting her eyebrows together. "What'd he do?"

"Dropped in on my wave and kicked me in the face," I elaborate.

"It was accidental," McKayla assures her.

"Sally, can you get us the signups for Junior Champs, Pipeline and regionals?" Papaw interjects before this can get any uglier.

"Of course," she replies. She shoots me a look. It appears sweetly curious, but it's the kind of sweet that you cannot get without a dash of devilishness. "Back in the game, Annie?"

"If no one kills me before I can get on my board," I joke. She laughs exaggeratedly and hands me the papers, which I begin to fill out.

Sally organizes papers as Papaw reads the regionals pamphlet and I work through the forms, consulting Papaw on what events to go for. McKayla picks up a magazine and begins to read. Finally, I finish and give them back to Sally, who stows them in a folder. "You're good to go," she replies. "See you there." Great. First competition in a week. Let's hope the skateboarding and snowboarding in New York pays off. Bonus if I can kick Sally Emerson's butt (which I totally can).

Sally thinks she's the best surfer girl on Oahu, but she's delusional. She's good, but she's never been the best. No matter how popular she is at the mall or in school, that's no advantage out in the ocean. She and I have been pitted against each other since my first competition when I was 5. I won, of course. She came in second, and has hated me ever since. McKayla's gotten better since then, so she's not particularly fond of her either, but she hates my guts. She doesn't like anyone who can one-up her, and I have every time I've been here to compete.

"Can I go back out now?" I plead. Papaw laughs.

"No, I think it'd be best to keep that on ice a little longer," he responds, gesturing at my eye. I make a fake pouty face and cross my arms, but he just laughs again.

After bidding Sally goodbye and driving home, McKayla decides to go back out on the waves. "Gotta get a jump on the competition," she says, winking. I laugh and head back to my room, calling a hello to Grammy on the way.

FIVE

I crash on my bed, crank up the stereo and select Mayday Parade's version of "Somebody That I Used to Know" on my computer. Using my one good eye and holding a new ice pack on the other, I scroll through Twitter. Amy's already posted a ton of photos from camping with Logan. It looks like she's having a blast. I pull out my iPhone and take the ice off my bruise to capture a selfie. Ouch. Now I know why people have been so shocked all day. The bruise is dark purple with blue around the edges, encompassing my entire right eye socket and a bit below. It does not look pretty, to say the least.

I snap a quick photo and add the caption "1st day back in Oahu. Surfing, got kicked in the eye, suffice to say, my day has been interesting. #trainingmishaps." Tweet. I continue to scroll, until the little device buzzes with a text from Amy. "So… Logan kissed me at the campfire a few minutes ago…" I roll my eyes, but text back "Aww sweet :) congrats. Loved seeing your pics on Twitter."

It's not that I hate love. I don't. In fact, I frequently read love stories and watch all those chick flick romantic comedies. Jane Austen is one of my favorite authors, and pretty much all she ever wrote was romance. It's just that I know that's what they are: stories. Fiction. Love like that is too good to be true, and I don't want my best friends getting hurt because they're mistaken that it is true.

Speaking of stories, I pull the sequel to *This Present Darkness* off my bedside table and try to read with my one eye. Unfortunately, I can't wear my glasses with the ice pack and it's a pain reading with the one eye. I don't need glasses all the time, but I depend on them heavily for up close reading or working on the computer. Well, scrap that idea.

I turn off the music and pick up the guitar in the corner. A beautiful instrument, made of all Koa wood, a gorgeous Hawaiian wood that almost all surfboards used to be made out of, and some still are. It's my favorite out of the three I have. I have my favorite acoustic that stays at my dad's house most of the time, a black Fender

Strat and amplifier at my mom's house and a black Taylor acoustic at my mom's house.

My left hand fingers skim over the neck and my right hand hits the strings, damping them slightly and start playing "Before He Cheats" by Carrie Underwood. Sometimes, a good Carrie Underwood breakup song is the only way to let out frustration. Even if you haven't broken up with anyone, they're still great for letting off steam.

After a little more guitar, I hop up and head out to the living room, taking my pillow with me. Browsing the DVD case, I'm in the mood for an old favorite. Something to cheer me up. "What are you thinking?" Grammy asks, settling into the couch. I hold up the case for the 2005 *Pride and Prejudice* starring Keira Knightly and Matthew MacFayden, based on the Jane Austen novel. She smiles. "Good idea," she replies as I slide the disc into the player.

"I love this movie," I sigh. She nods.

"How's your eye?" she inquires. I shrug and take the ice off for her to see. She inspects it and nods.

"Sawyer gave you quite the bruise," she states. "You really can't hold this against him, though. He's as sweet a young man as you'll ever meet." I laugh.

"You know the phrase 'adding insult to injury?'" I inquire. She nods and I point at my eye. "He added injury to insult." She laughs that familiar musical laugh I love.

"I'm serious, though. He's a very nice boy," she remarks after she's stopped laughing.

"I'm sure he is," I retort. "When he's not dropping in on other people's waves and kicking them in the face."

"Yes," she laughs again. I lay back with my legs over her lap and hold the ice to my face, watching Elizabeth Bennet's tale of the ups and downs of her and her sisters' love lives unfold for the next two hours in front of my eyes. Well, eye.

After the movie, she heads into the kitchen and I decide to sit at the bar so I can keep talking to her. "So what's new in the world of Andrea?"

"Not much," I reply. "School year was good. Read a lot. Read, like, the best book ever."

"What book?" she asks, wiping down the counter and preparing to make dinner.

"*Three Hours Too Soon*," I sigh. "Lots of great lines, great love story, very tragic."

"Maybe I'll read it," she supposes.

"Movie comes out the day before Junior Champs," I add. "If you want to read it, read it before then. I probably won't be able to shut up about it after going to see it."

"Maybe I'll just go see the movie then," teases Grammy, winking. She and I have a thing for reading the book before watching the movie. The only thing I don't read before I see it is Shakespeare and that's because it's easier to follow the story line if you can see what's happening instead of just reading the script. Boy, kids at school drove me nuts about that when *The Hunger Games* came out. Almost none of them read the books, so, of course, they missed nearly half the details of the plot line.

"I'm excited for competition," I state. My fingers start to trail around the counter in various patterns.

"Good. How often did you skate back north?"

"Every day, or as close to it as I could get," I reply. "A lot of the local skaters taught me new tricks that I can't wait to try on the water."

"Sawyer skates, too," she informs me. "He competes at surfing and apparently used to snowboard back in Australia during the winter."

"Cool," I reply absentmindedly. "I kind of figured he did. He was doing skating tricks before he kicked me in the face."

"So do you really not like him?" Grammy asks.

"Grammy, he kicked me in the face," I respond shortly.

"Yes, but I hit you in the face on accident and knocked out your loose tooth when you were ten," she points out. "And you still like me."

"That's different," I argue. "That was an accident and you're my grandma."

"You really think he meant to kick you?" she asks skeptically.

"No, but he dropped in on my wave on purpose," I explain. "The kick in the face was a byproduct of that."

"Sweetheart, he got too close and couldn't correct the mistake before it was too late. He didn't see you," she defends. I huff and hop down off the barstool, climbing over the back of the couch to lay back again. I know he didn't really mean to kick me, but the thought of letting him get off easy after dropping in on my wave makes me want to keel over and die. And the whole "it wasn't my fault you almost drowned" thing doesn't exactly boost his position on my "People I Like" list. It does, however, raise him a few places above Sally Emerson and just below Veronica Roth on my "People I Want to Punch in the Face" list. I'm sorry, but *Divergent*? Immense wasted potential. Great first book. I thought it could recover from the second book in the trilogy and get better, but boy, was I wrong.

Regardless of my aggravation with authors who missed the "Unless Your Name is Shakespeare, Don't Kill Your Main Characters" memo, Sawyer Hensley is not on my good side right now.

The steady rhythm of my grandmother's knife chopping pineapple on her wooden cutting board pounds away as I pick up my phone and scroll through Twitter again. Nothing new. Instead, I switch to Instagram, glancing at my friends' photos intermixed with my favorite celebrities' pictures. Taylor Swift's cat did something adorable; Harry Styles took a random photo; Michael Clifford dyed his hair again; the usual. Social media. What would we do without it?

Grammy calls Papaw in to dinner a little later from the garage. Did I mention my Papaw restores old motorcycles? He spends most of the day in the garage, fixing up old pieces of junk into well-oiled vintage beauties. Hands coated in grease, he immediately heads to the kitchen sink. "Why can't you get scrubs that smell like seawater or motor oil?" Papaw questions, using the "Vanilla Breeze" sugar scrub to get the black goo off his hands.

"Because you get enough of that on your hands as it is," Grammy replies plainly, her eyes twinkling. I smile, happy to watch the playful banter between my grandparents. I envy them sometimes. My grandparents are among the lucky few that got it right.

I suppose I'll amend my earlier statement: True love doesn't exist anymore. Back before "love" meant two people making googly eyes at each other, it worked. They paid attention to each other's personalities, quirks and other things that matter so much more than appearance. My grandparents were best friends for three years before he asked her out. By then, they knew what made each other tick. She knew he had a passion for fixing up old things and making them new again. He knew she loved pre-1900s history. True love existed back then because their generation was smart. My generation just wants to have a good time with no strings attached. Unfortunately, that means girls with standards end up as old cat ladies, or divorced and trying to drown the pain in something else, whether it be work, drugs, alcohol or other men. It might not be pretty, but it's true.

Grammy brings a large pot over and I smell one of the best scents known to man: My grandmother's Char-siu. It's a Chinese version of barbecue pulled pork with a sweet and tangy Hawaiian glaze and a slice of pineapple on Hawaiian rolls. Hawaiian rolls are the best bread on the face of the earth. Sourdough is close second, but Hawaiian rolls have a sweet flavor that goes with anything and nothing can match. Yet another thing my New Yorker friends didn't understand about me. Amy still swears that New York style pizza is better (but that's unfair because it's pizza. Pizza trumps all).

"Annie? Would you like to pray?" Grammy asks. I shrug.

"Sure," I reply. They bow their heads and outstretch their hands toward each other and me. I do the same, linking hands with each of them, and try to come up with a decent prayer. "Lord Jesus, thank you for today. Thank you for bringing me back home to be with Grammy and Papaw. Thank you for this wonderful food Grammy made. Please bless it and let it nourish us to serve you. Amen." They echo my last word and dig in to the food.

Honestly, I don't really know what I believe. My parents and grandparents are Christians, but I don't really know where I fit. I don't get it. A God that loves and protects and all that wouldn't let me get caught in the cross-fire of the fight between my parents, right? Well, here I am. What's up, God? Still working on that plan? I could use some instruction right about now. Or anytime between now and ten years ago would've been nice.

"So, training," Papaw starts. I listen attentively while chewing the most delicious thing in the world. "I'd say we'll go on dawn patrol and get up at six-thirty and get you to Sunset, a ways down from Pipeline."

Sunset is Sunset Beach, which starts at the notorious Banzai Pipeline and goes on for about two miles. It's one of the spots where the Vans Triple Crown of Surfing competition is held in the winter. Unfortunately, summer break happens during summer. The best big waves happen in the winter, so all the big competitions are in the fall and winter. It's also where the Oahu Junior Championships are held, so I'll be competing there in a week.

"Sounds good," I say, nodding. "What do I do about my eye though? Can the saltwater hurt it worse?"

"Power through your training and I'll give you some drops to put in when you get back. You can ice it, too," Grammy consoles. I nod.

"Since I didn't stay to watch you yesterday, I'll just let you do what you like for a few waves and see where we should start with training," Papaw suggests. I nod again, alternating between excitement about surfing and utter bliss over Grammy's Char-siu.

After dinner consists of my doing the dishes, Grammy wiping down the kitchen counters and Papaw flipping channels until he finds some news program to watch. As interesting as this is, I decide to go to my room and see if my parents have any time for me whatsoever.

Upon viewing the gorgeous floral environment outside my back sliding door, I opt to head out there instead of flop on my bed. Settling down in the beach chair just outside my sliding door, I debate who to call first while listening to the far-off sound of the waves. I settle on Dad, because he's in my same time zone, so he's most likely done with work, or as done with work as is physically possible for my father.

Punching in the numbers, I hit "Call" and wait. He answers on the first ring. "Hey, surfer girl, how's it hanging?" he inquires. I laugh, wondering what my dad's clients would think if they heard him talking like a surfer.

"Hanging loose, Dad," I shoot back. "How is it up on the mainland?"

"Oh, business as usual," he sighs. "Lots of meetings, just winning over a high-profile client."

"As much fun as that sounds, I'm stuck here. I start training for competition tomorrow," I inform him.

"Annie, you didn't say anything about competition! That's awesome!" he answers. I actually did say something about competition. A lot of somethings, as a matter of fact. Is it bad that I barely notice what my dad forgets about our conversations anymore? Practically everything I say is apparently not worthy of his attention or memory.

"Thanks," I say instead. "I'm excited. I'm signed up for two local competitions and, depending on the results from those, I might have a shot at regionals."

"Your mother agreed to regionals?" he asked. "That uncharacteristic of her."

"We're not certain about it yet," I dodge, trying to weave my way around the question. "Right now, I'm just focusing on my first competition in a few years."

"Well, you were pretty good at skateboarding and snowboarding competition," he rationalizes. "I doubt being in your natural element will hurt you."

"I know," I reply. "It is different though, and I'm nervous."

"Well, hang in there, hon. I've gotta go. My assistant is calling me."

"All right. Love you, Dad," I bid.

"Love you too," he says, hanging up.

Before I call my mother, I simply put my head back, close my eyes and listen to the rustling of the palm trees. The warm breeze washes over my face and I take a deep breath, smelling the fragrant Hawaiian flowers drifting on the salty breeze. This is my favorite feeling. Relaxed, warm with a little wind touching my cheeks, devoid of cares or worries. The feeling of being home.

Next, I tap in my mom's number and wait for the rings to end. Just as I think her voice mail is about to begin, she answers. "Hi sweetheart!" she says. "How's my girl?"

"Good," I reply. "I signed up for those competitions I mentioned today."

"Fun," she sighs. "How's McKayla?"

"She's good. She has a boyfriend," I answer.

"How sweet," Mom replies quaintly. "You should invite a boy from your school over sometime this fall. Or maybe that snowboarder you used to train with—Jake, right?"

"Mom, the guys at my school are idiots," I respond matter-of-factly. "And Jake moved to Colorado to train for the Olympics."

"Have you met any boys on the island yet?" she inquires.

"Two. One is nice, but his little brother is a jerk."

"How old is he?"

"The little brother is my age and the nice one is twenty," I remember.

"Are they cute?"

"Mo-om!" I whine.

"Sorry," she laughs. "I just can't help it! I want to see my baby fall in love someday."

"I can't make guys fall for me mom," I say, trying to avoid explaining the hideous truth to her again. "If they like me, they like me. If they don't, they don't. I can't do anything about it."

"Except go out with them if they do like you."

"Mom!"

"Sorry, honey," she laughs again. "Alright, I've gotta go. Client calling."

"Okay. Love you mom."

"Love you too." Dead line. I sigh.

I've explained the whole "I don't believe in love" thing to Mom before. She just doesn't get it. It's incomprehensible to her that a hormonal teenager would be able to resist going after every other boy she sees. I think she feels bad, too. She wants me to fall in love because she feels like it's her fault that I believe this. Like she can somehow erase the pain of the divorce by getting me to fall in love.

"Why is life so complicated?!" I shout at the flowers. Sadly, no one can answer that question.

I pop inside to grab my book and settle back into my chair. I disappear into the world of *This Present Darkness*'s riveting sequel and don't come out until Grammy taps my shoulder, telling me it's almost ten and she's going to bed. I nod and yawn, following her inside to ready myself for bed. I have to be well-rested for tomorrow morning to pull out all the stops.

“Alright, I don’t want you to hold back,” Papaw instructs the next morning. I dig my toes further into the hot sand as I nod. The warmth of the sun filters through my rash guard, heating up my shoulders. “I want everything. New tricks, old tricks, whatever. Be careful on that knee, too. Clean rides, okay?”

“Got it,” I affirm.

“Go,” he commands, nodding towards the waves. I run out into the water and let the waves wash over my legs as I dive onto my board, paddling out. The water is crystal clear, so clear, I can see straight down to the ocean floor. My eye doesn't bother me too much, but the water does sting more than usual.

I do as Papaw instructed and pull some radical tricks on my first wave. My bad knee hurts a little, but nothing I can't handle. Maria, my physical therapist back in New York, cleared me for surfing before I left, so I'm not worried.

"Good. Not great, but good," my grandpa says as I paddle into shore. "Try a slob air reverse after a vertical backhand snap." I hold up a thumbs-up in reply.

Once back in the lineup, I wait for a wave. It doesn't take long for one to come my way, and the pop is smooth. The pop is when a surfer stands up on a wave. I turn the nose of my board straight up and swerve forward, then prepare for the air. As I lift off the wave, I grab the toe-side edge of my board, positioning the board so my tail is behind me. I pull the board in close to my body, then let go as I turn to drop. The exhilaration of a jump always makes me feel super-human.

As I hit the water again, I pull a 360 degree carve for good measure and toss up a sick amount of spray. That's one thing I like about surfing that snowboarding and skateboarding don't have. I can't carve in skateboarding, and when I carve in snowboarding, it looks really cool when the snow blows up around me, but it's just not the same. I can't feel the water droplets hitting my skin. I can't feel the film of water wash over my toes as my board cuts through the wave. It doesn't feel like gliding on nothing.

"Choka!" he yells. "Go for a little more air next time and try some clidro!"

"Okay!" I shout back. Surfer lingo lesson #4,248,109: Clidro is swerving back and forth on a wave while riding down the line.

I try the same combination again, only with some clidro thrown in in between the jump and the 360 carve. Papaw waves me in and I fly in with the next wave, riding it to shore. "Nice to see your skating and snowboarding paid off," he says, nodding. "I think you're really ready to take on this competition."

"Really?" I inquire, extremely pleased.

"Oh, without a doubt," he replies. "Not many seventeen year old girls can throw down a wave like that and keep their technique from going out the window, while still adding their own style. That was great. I would work on perfecting the hardest moves you can do, and start trying some new stuff too over the week. Just play around. This first competition will be all about evaluating you." My grandpa doesn't just throw out compliments when it comes to surfing, so clear-ly, I'm doing better than I thought.

He stays for a little while longer to watch me surf, commenting occasionally, then heads out when McKayla arrives around 10AM. "So much for getting a head start on the competition, huh?" I yell as she paddles out into the lineup.

"You always were the dawn patrol girl," she shouts back over the waves.

Having Papaw here is helpful for perfecting my technique, but when it comes to pushing me, no one beats McKayla. We surfed our first waves together a long time ago and even then, we were competitive. "That all you got?" I shout as she completes a kickflip, which is a 360° spin in the air, landing back on the wave.

"All I'm hearing is a lot of big talk," she shouts. "All I'm seeing is a shubie."

In response, I snag the next wave and start with another kickflip. From there, I add a little clidro, add a 360° shove-it where I spin the board around under my feet, and a layback, named such because when performing the trick, I lean back on the wave and snap the lip while my body lays horizontally. It's hard for most surfers, but thanks to a lot of time in the half pipe, I'm used to laying back to perform tricks and my leg and core strength is such that I can perform it well. I flash her a little smile when I sit up on my board, back in the lineup.

"Shut up," she quips, not looking at me. I smirk.

"How're your legs holding up?" I inquire smugly. "Because with how many waves you've caught, you should have some pretty little surfer's knots by now."

"Ha ha, very funny," she retorts. Surfer's knots are little swollen spots of tissue on your ankles and knees you get when you kneel for a long time on your board because you haven't caught a wave in a while.

She paddles in to the next wave that comes, pulling a clean ride. She adds a little snap at the end and loses her footing, going down instantly.

"Wipeout!" I shout, laughing. She comes back up and gives me the evil eye.

"Somehow that was your fault!" she shouts.

"How was that my fault?!" I yell back defensively, stifling a laugh.

"I don't know," she replies, mounting her board. "But it was! Somehow!" I collapse into a fit of laughter and shove her shoulder, to which she shoves me. I shove her back and she shoves me off my board. Oh, she's gonna get it now. Plunged under the water, I swim over and gently brush her leg with my arm.

I take my leash off so as not to disturb my board, then give the board a good hard yank, like they do in all those shark attack movies when a surfer gets bitten. I jerk it around a bit and then let it go entirely, as if the leash has been bitten off by a Great White. I brush up against her leg again, then grab hold and pull her under. I swim up to the surface and immediately burst into laughter. McKayla isn't particularly terrified of sharks, but she wouldn't want keep one for a pet in the bathtub, either. Every surfer should at least be wary of their surroundings.

"ANDREA KALANI MAVERICK," she shouts upon surfacing. I put on my leash, ready to go. "Get over her so I can drag you down to a real shark!"

"Catch me if you can!" I call back, paddling into the next wave.

"Oh, I don't doubt I can," she yells. I laugh, pulling a few tricks to taunt her and then bail out, diving off my board, and come up to watch her sail past me. Oh, it's good to be home.

SEVEN

"This is going to be the best movie ever!" McKayla states excitedly. I laugh.

"Wait, wait, wait! Here, come here," I instruct, seeing the poster for *Three Hours Too Soon*. "Grammy, here, can you take a picture?" I ask, handing her my phone and posing with Mac. She takes a few good ones and a few silly ones and hands it back to me as we continue into the movie theater. "Thanks."

"So what did you think of the book, Mrs. Maverick?" McKayla inquires.

"I loved it," Grammy answers. "I thought it was brilliant."

"I can't wait to see what made the cut," I comment. "I mean, Adam Reed seemed excited about it, so it can't be that bad, right?"

"Hello, Caleb Daniels and Allison Grantz. How could be bad with those two?" Mac questions.

"A fantastic question that will be answered in three hours," I reply, stepping into the line to buy tickets. "Three for *Three Hours Too Soon*, please." I glance around as the woman behind the counter prints our tickets. The only people that seem to be standing around are those who are waiting in line for snacks.

On the opposite wall is a large *Three Hours Too Soon* display, with Caleb and Allison's faces enlarged on either side. Brown-haired, blue-eyed Caleb image reminds me of another brown-haired, blue-eyed boy who has made himself scarce since the day he gave me the lovely bruise that has stuck around for almost a week now. Five days, actually. It doesn't hurt as bad as it did that first day, but it hasn't gotten any better in the looks department. On the upside, I'll look tough tomorrow.

Mac and I would've gone to an earlier showing, but we were out on the waves, throwing down a serious practice to get on Sally Emerson's nerves. The three of us coincidentally picked the same surf spot to practice at today. Sally's good, but, not to be cocky or anything, Mac and I can take her any day, so we stuck around and showed off as long as we could.

"$32.10," the ticket woman replies, handing me the tickets. I hand her the money and take the tickets. "Theater eleven, to your right." We step to the side to sort out the tickets and let the next customers step forward.

"Two to *Three Hours Too Soon*," a familiar voice requests. Great. I though I wasn't going to have to put up with him until tomorrow.

"Sawyer! Melissa!" Grammy greets, surprised.

"Ellie!" the woman beside Sawyer Jerkface Hensley exclaims. "Great minds think alike, I suppose!"

"Yes, they do," Grammy replies.

"Hey, McKayla. Hi Annie," Sawyer greets. "Guys, this is my mum. Mum, you've met McKayla Atwood and this is Andrea Maverick, the girl I told you about." I smile and shake her outstretched hand, then turn to McKayla.

"Mac, come on," I command. "Let's go get snacks."

"Oh, honey, you can go with your friends if you'd like," Mrs. Hensley tells Sawyer. Sawyer smiles, kisses her on the cheek and then follows us as I turn and pull McKayla towards the snack bar. The line has basically disappeared, but unfortunately, so has my appetite.

"One large cherry/blue raspberry swirl Icee," I say at the counter. The twenty-something boy behind the counter rings up my order and hands me the large cup, which, to my excitement, is a reusable *Three Hours Too Soon* cup. McKayla and Sawyer both order the same, but Mac gets Skittles and Sawyer adds Sour Patch Kids to his order. Mrs. Hensley and Grammy meet up with us as we head to theater eleven.

"So, Sawyer, did you read the book?" asks McKayla. He nods. "I don't usually, but my little sister and my mum read it and said it was really good, so I picked it up and couldn't stop until I was done," he answers. "Best book I've read in a while."

"Cool," Mac returns. We enter the theater and begin to climb the stairs up to the middle row. Grammy and Mrs. Hensley go first, and I try to squeeze past them to sit next to Grammy and Mac, but Grammy stops me.

"Go sit with Sawyer. I'll be fine," she says, smiling. She might be fine, but I won't be.

I do as my grandmother says, though, and take a seat to Mac's right, next to Sawyer. We just sort of sit there for a moment in awkward silence, then a movie trivia question pops up on the screen. "I love these," he comments. "'What Broadway actress and singer best known as the Wicked Witch of the West in *Wicked* co-stared in the Disney movie *Frozen*?'"

"Idina Menzel," we answer in sync, even before the multiple choice answers pop up. He glances at me just as I glance at him and we both look down in embarrassment.

"My sister loves that movie," he explains. "I can't go five minutes without hearing the soundtrack. Before I'd seen the movie, I'd heard the Demi Lovato version of 'Let It Go' on the radio and when she mentioned the song, I said 'Oh, that one by Demi Lovato?' She about went nuts, ranting about how the Idina Menzel one was the real one."

"I sort of... did that to my dad once..." I mumble sheepishly. "My mom and I are huge *Wicked* fans though. We've seen her on Broadway twice. It gives me chills when she sings 'Defying Gravity.' She just has a range like no other."

"Cool," he replies, smiling. Suddenly another one pops up. *What roles did Ansel Elgort and Shaliene Woodley, lead roles of* The Fault in Our Stars, *play in the film* Divergent?

Sawyer furrows his brow at the screen, exclaiming "Shoot! I know this!"

I smile and answer "Caleb and Beatrice Prior, brother and sister" confidently and even a little bit smugly. Who said movie trivia is useless?

Mac pounds her fist on the armrest on my other side and exclaims "Dang it! How'd I miss that?" I laugh. Sawyer glances at me with a devious smirk on his face and suddenly, we are competing just as hard as we will be tomorrow at Junior Champs. By the time the previews start, I've gotten ten out of eleven, and he's gotten eight out of eleven. (For the record, the one I missed was about an actor in a movie I have not seen and do not care to.)

The previews play on forever as they always do, and then finally, the movie begins. As the story of Jane Thompson and Lucas Blake unfolds, I become unaware of my surroundings and lose myself in the story right up to the very end, even though I'm bawling my eyes out. The screen goes black and the lights come up as the credits play. I sigh and wipe my eyes. McKayla does the same beside me, and I hear a sniffle come from on my right. I quickly glance at Sawyer. Is it just my own eyes adjusting to the light and being full of water or are his eyes slightly red? "Were you crying?" I ask before I can stop myself.

"Are you sure I didn't impair your vision last week?" he asks defensively. "No, I wasn't crying." I turn away and roll my eyes. Yeah, sure. I've said it before and I'll say it again: Jerkface.

The five of us stand up and file out of the theater, Sawyer staying fairly quiet as Mac and I chatter away about how cute Jane and Lucas are, how cute Caleb Daniels is and how awesome Adam Reed is. In the parking lot, the Hensleys start to head for their car as we head for ours, but as I turn away from bidding them goodbye, Sawyer exclaims "Wait!" and grabs my hand. I remove it from his grasp immediately, but his hands are soft and I almost regret letting go a moment later. Almost. But I did let go, which reassures me I have not yet completely lost my mind. "Good luck tomorrow," he says. "Both of you. Just, you know, in case I don't see you tomorrow before you compete."

"You too," Mac returns. I nod in agreement.

"See you tomorrow," he bids, waving.

"See you," I answer. Thirty minutes later, I'm lying in bed, trying to fall asleep and still thinking about Sawyer's hand. Weird, I know. I have tried everything from replaying *Three Hours Too Soon* in my head to finishing *Piercing the Darkness*, but I just can't get that stupid hand-grab thing out of my head. I don't even know what it was. His hand was softer then you'd expect. It felt kind of like your skin feels after a paraffin wax dip at the spa.

I try to shake it off and tell myself that it doesn't matter what his hands feel like, because all I need to know about him is 1. I can beat him in surfing and 2. I can beat him at movie trivia. Other than that, I stand by my earlier statements: His name might as well be Sawyer Jerkface Hensley.

EIGHT

The first thing that hits my ears the next morning is the opening notes of "Madhouse" by Little Mix. As I'm about to hit snooze, a thought pops into my head: *Today is Junior Champs.* Suddenly, my feet hit the floor and I'm blasting my "Pre-Competition" playlist, beginning with same song I chose for my alarm. The beat floods in through my ears and seeps into my veins, pumping my heart with excitement. I jump around a bit to loosen up, then change out of my pajamas and into my black bikini. Instead of a rash guard, I throw on a t-shirt and a pair of comfy cotton shorts. I'll get a competition rash guard at the beach today that's a certain color and has my number on it, so the judges can identify me out in the lineup.

The way the competition works is extremely similar to a swim meet, if you know what that is. Each surfer is put in one or two categories, called divisions, usually by age and gender. Each event has several rounds. The Junior Champs events have four rounds: Qualifying, Quarter Finals, Semi Finals and Finals. Each round is a series of heats, where a certain amount of competitors make it through to the next round. During qualifiers, the top thirty surfers make it through. In quarter finals, the top fifteen make it, and five of those fifteen make it through the semi finals to the finals. Those five battle it out for the top three spots to place.

Typically, there's about four or five surfers per heat, so naturally, elimination is the longest round due to how many heats are scheduled and competitors signed up.

Bigger competitions take place over five or six days, because each heat takes about twenty to thirty minutes. Junior Champs is today and tomorrow, with qualifiers this morning and the rest of the rounds tomorrow most likely. I'm in the girls 15-18 event and the girls 17-18 event. They only do the large-spectrum event for the 15-18 girls and 15-18 boys, because most of us are on the same skill level thanks to the fact that we've all been surfing since we could stand up. Some work at it more than others. To some, it's a recreational sport and a chance to hang out with friends. For others, it's a career path.

Me? I take it pretty darn seriously. Anyway, each surfer is allowed ten waves per heat and only the top three waves count towards that surfer's final score for the heat. Each wave is scored from 0.5 to 10, 0.5 being you managed to get your feet on the board and straighten up, 10 being a perfectly executed ride.

Like how some mainland cities revolve around baseball or basketball, Oahu revolves around surfing. It's the most common sport kids participate in, but unlike most kids' sports, all the local new channels around here cover the bigger events. The last time I competed, I was fifteen and on a two-week winter break from school in New York and won both big competitions I was in. I compete a bunch in the winter in New York with snowboarding, too, but this is different. A few local news stations already caught wind of me being back and have been guessing about what competitions I'll be in, if any. This is in front of basically the whole island I grew up on.

With my fluorescent green surfboard and canvas hobo bag in tow, I slide on my rubber slippers and head out to the kitchen. I grab a dragon fruit-flavored Vitamin Water and a few protein bars for my bag to bring along, then sit down to drink the smoothie Grammy has ready for me. "Ready?" Papaw asks. I run through a quick checklist in my head before I respond: We looked at the forecast last night and the conditions look prime; My bag is packed up with my phone, headphones, surf wax and anything else I could possibly need; Grammy's well-trained fingers start in on french braiding my hair, so all I've got to do is check in when I get there.

"Stoked," I reply.

"Good," he says, nodding. After both my hair and breakfast are finished, Papaw takes my board out and straps it to the roof of the beater. Papaw, Grammy and I load up and move out, reaching the beach ten minutes later. We pile out of the car, unhook the board and follow the other teens carrying their boards onto the sand. At the sign in table, I sign in, get my shirt (pink, number 15), quickly find McKay-la and pull her towards a spot on the shore.

Her parents and my grandparents follow us and set down their chairs and bags and other random stuff. We throw down our boards and before I can even get my surf wax out, I hear shouting and five local reporters and their camera men or photographers rush over to us. I stand and smile at them.

"Andrea! Welcome back to Oahu," one woman greets. I'd hate to have to wear what these people have to wear to cover a surf compe-tition. Heels and a women's dress suit? Heck no.

"Thank you," I reply. "I'm excited to be home!"

"What happened to your eye?" someone else inquires.

"During my first day of training, another surfer dropped in on my wave and when he cut in front of me, he kicked me in the face," I explain.

"What surfer?"

"Sawyer Hensley," I answer nonchalantly.

"How have you kept up your surfing while away?" another re-porter interrogates.

"I've been competing at snowboarding in the winter in New York and I skateboard wherever I am," I answer. "I take tricks from all three sport and adapt them for each terrain. I guess that's why everyone says I have such an individualized style."

"How you do hope to place today?"

"Honestly, I just came to do my best and evaluate where I stand. I know I've got some stiff competition and I'm excited to see how I size up," I respond.

"Is it true that since your last competition, you took on world-famous big wave spot, Mavericks?" a man inquires.

"It is true," I reply. "I've now actually surfed it twice, since typically I stay near the spot with my dad in the summer."

"What made you come back here?" Channel 3's correspondent asks.

"I missed my true home," I reply honestly. "Oahu is my favorite place in the world and nothing can ever change that." With that, I wave them away and kneel down to start waxing my board.

"Look at you miss Celebrity," Mac laughs.

"It's nice to know everybody missed me!" I reply. I pause and peel my shirt off to let the sun shine on my skin.

"Mind if we camp here?" an Aussie accent asks behind me.

"Not at all," I say, rolling my eyes and turning to Sawyer. He's already got his rash guard on. The royal blue compliments his skin tone and eyes nicely. A girl about thirteen stands behind him with her white number twenty-seven rash guard on and pink board under her arm. "Who's this?"

"My sister, Julia," he introduces. "Julia, this is Andrea and McKayla."

"Hi Julia," I greet, smiling. She smiles shyly and says a soft "hi" in return, before turning to her mother, asking her something and running off towards a group of other young girls. "So you're all surfers are you?" I say quizzically.

"Better believe it," Sawyer replies. "Actually, we're real surfers. We make our own boards instead of surfing with those pop-outs you junkyard dogs use." A junkyard dog is a surfer that has bad technique and goes for bad waves. Instead of going off at the jerkface and saying the choice words I'd like to, I smirk and raise my eyebrows.

"Real surfers, huh? Must be pretty nice boards," I reply cooly. "I suppose you have to be snake too to be 'real surfer'?"

"I stand by my earlier statements," he defends. "I miscalculated and got too close to stop."

"Well, I suppose we'll see who the junkyard dog is by tomorrow, won't we?" I say, finishing off the waxing and grabbing the heat sheet from Grammy. "Do you have my rash guard?" I inquire sharply, still ruffled by his insult. She hands it to me and I stretch it over my head and take my shorts off.

"Who stuck a bee in your bonnet?" Grammy asks.

"Sawyer," I inform her.

"What'd he do?"

"Said I wasn't a real surfer and called me a junkyard dog," I reply, oddly hurt. I suppose an insult hurts, no matter who it's from.

"He also said my board was a pop-out."

"Well then," she says. "Prove him wrong." I smile.

"Oh, don't worry. He's got one heck of a shock coming," I reply with a smirk.

I'm heat two out of eleven for the 15-18 girls division, which goes at the same time as the boys, then I have to wait for the 17-18 boys to go. The 15-16 boys and girls will go at the same time as the 17-18 surfers because of the way the beach is sectioned off for the competition. The under 15 divisions are on another area of the beach. Since it's almost two miles long, the surf can be totally different at one end then it is at the other, and most often, it is. With the 15-18 event starting now at eight AM, we'll be done with that by about 12:30 PM. The 17-18 boys will go after that until about 5, then the girls will go until about ten o'clock tonight. Suffice it to say, competitions are exhausting.

Heat one of the girls aren't bad. One takes a nasty spill a few waves in and can't shake it, though. I just watch, as that's all I can do. I won't know where I stand until much later in the heats. This heat's on the short end, at just twenty minutes. Over the loudspeaker, I hear them announce my heat and I go line up next to the four other girls I'm surfing with. The alarm sounds and we dive in, paddling out to the lineup.

Once out, I sit up and wait for a wave. I let three of the other girls battle it out over the first wave and take a slightly bigger one that rolls around a minute later. I remember my strategy: assure a decent spot, but don't show off or make myself a target.

I start the ride with a nice bottom turn, a move to get me into position, a solid 360° carve, then a 180° carve landing backwards and snapping the lip off the top to face forward again. With another 360° carve, I finish out the wave and paddle back into the lineup. Honestly, this is just warm up. No big deal. Unless I get disqualified or don't do anything but stand up on my other waves, I'm fine.

I get two more clean waves, which score decently, then a third when I show a bit of what's to come. Papaw and I agreed, no slob air reverse or layback until tomorrow, so today's pretty easy. 360° carves, a few 180° airs, clidro, vertical backhand snaps and a lot of slashing. The next nine heats make my serious competition today pretty clear: Sally Emerson, McKayla, an eighteen-year-old named Kara Vanderbilt, and an eighteen-year-old named Paige LeGroe. I end the morning in spot number fifteen. Dead last of the qualifiers. Sawyer ended up in spot number one. I shoot him a glance and a smile upon hearing the results. "I guess junkyard dogs just don't score well, huh?" he says with a satisfied smirk.

"We'll see," I retort, wondering what his face will look like tomorrow. With that I turn away and debate with Grammy, Papaw and the Atwoods what to get for lunch.

Eventually, we settled on sending Papaw, Mr. Hensley and Mr. Atwood to Tara's, a beachside shack run by Tara Adams and her family. Four words: Best. Tuna. Salad. Ever. I kid you not, I didn't even like fish before I went to Tara's. Goldfish crackers were as close as I was going to get to liking the actual things that swim in the water until I had her stuff.

Anyway, they bring us back lunch and we all sit and talk strategy. "That was smart, not making yourself a target," Mac says. "Sitting in third, I'm not fooling anyone what my skill level is, especially the judges."

"This next one, do the same thing. There's less girls, so put a little more out there, but again, not enough to make yourself a threat," Papaw instructs. "That was good, sticking to 180 airs. Don't go for 360 or big airs until tomorrow." I nod and glance at Sally, who's laughing with a group of other surfers and shoots me a look that, to anyone else would appear a sweet look, but there's an underlying hate to the sweetness that makes me roll my eyes and turn back to everyone else.

A bit later, I see Sawyer heading down to the edge of the waves, getting ready for his heat. As I watch him surf, McKayla comes up behind me and comments "Told you he was good." I don't reply. I hate to admit it, but he's more than good. He's amazing.

Papaw and Grammy take me home for a few hours to relax and rest up for the next event, then I'm back on the beach and in the water in heat five of the girls 17-18 division. I'm in the water with that Kara Vanderbilt, so obviously I have to kick it up a notch. Just as I'm about to step up my game, she loses her footing and takes some serious dirty lickings. Well, that stinks. Better today than tomorrow.

She recovers well, though. I have to watch out. She's in it to win it. With this in mind, I pull a clean ride that should score pretty well. The two of us battle for waves, but when I've got five good ones under my belt, I let her go for them. Play down my skill. Show off tomorrow. This is gonna be fun.

I come out of the water satisfied. The scores come and I'm twelfth. Mac is fourth. Sally's third, Kara's second and Paige LeGroe is first. "Aw, too bad," Sawyer remarks, coming up behind me as I pack up to leave. "Poor little gremmie. Good luck tomorrow."

"You too, kook," I return, not looking back. The sweet boy that cried during *Three Hours Too Soon* last night is gone and apparently has been replaced by a smack-talking jerk. Joke's on him when he sees my style tomorrow.

"Oh, my gosh," Mac says suddenly, covering her mouth after she's said it.

"What?" I inquire, puzzled.

"No. Just no," she laughs. "You'd kill me."

"Mac…" I say warily.

"Never mind," she giggles. "Just, don't worry about it."

"Has the saltwater gone to your brain, Mac?" I ask jokingly.

"I'm good," she says, still smiling uncontrollably. "See you tomorrow!"

"Yeah, see you tomorrow," I reply, raising an eyebrow at her. I laugh and shake my head, following Grammy to the car to head home and get some sleep. After all, I have to be well-rested to prove Jerkface wrong.

NINE

The next morning, I stand at the sign-in table picking up my day two heat sheet with Mac at my side. "Okay, you're heat one of six for quarters for 15-18," I tell her, flipping through the heat sheet. "And heat one of six for 17-18 quarters. I'm heat four for 15-18s and heat three for 17-18s." She marks hers down on her arm, then passes me the Sharpie. I do the same and stuff it in my bag, along with the papers. Once again, the Hensleys have camped out next to my grandparents and the Atwoods.

I sit down and take out my water bottle and *Mansfield Park* by Jane Austen, setting up for a good long wait before my heat. Like yesterday, the 15-18s will go before the 17-18s even start. Before I can start reading, though, they call Mac's heat and Sawyer's heat. I head down to a prime view spot to watch Mac.

As the horn sounds, Mac and her four competitors, including Sally Emerson, Paige LeGroe and Kara Vanderbilt, run into the water. The first one up for a wave is McKayla. She pulls off a good ride. Not stellar, but solid. When she's going for her third wave a few minutes later, Paige LeGroe drops in in front of her and snakes the wave out from right underneath her feet. Half the crowd and I groan simultaneously, while the other half cheer Paige on. It was a dirty trick, but not enough to get her disqualified.

I glance over to see Sawyer up on a wave, in the middle of a jump. He lands smoothly and finishes the wave with style. I'm going to have to pull out all the stops to impress this kid. I have an idea how, though.

There's a jump I've practiced a bit this week on the water called the Stalefish air reverse, in which I jump, then, as a regular footer (meaning I surf with my left foot forward), grab my heel-side rail (the edge to my back) with my right hand and spin either 180° or 360° in the air. It's a pro surf trick that I do all the time in the half pipe. It's how I've won several snowboarding competitions. I've been debating whether or not to pull it in finals. To give you an idea of the difficulty, pro surfers have won competitions with this move in certain combos.

Because the grab is so awkward, you have to be really coordinated to spin and hold the board at the same time. If I do it, it will be either as a hail-Mary play or just to show off if I've already cemented a win.

After Mac has finished, she's scored in third place again. Sawyer has kept his position in first. I wait for my heat to come along and when they call the heat before me, I wax my board. Guess I haven't explained that one yet, have I? Basically, you take a chunk of surf wax that looks a lot like a bar of soap and rub it all over the top of your board, coating it in wax. The wax gives you enough traction on the board to do things like shove-its, when you spin the board around under your feet, and snaps and keeps it from getting slick with water.

Next thing I know, I'm up. Papaw lays a hand on my shoulder just before the alarm sounds. "Remember not to just take any old wave. Wait for the good ones. It'll be worth it, trust me." I nod and the loud beep sounds over the speaker. I paddle out and kneel up on my board in the lineup, board pointed towards shore. The first wave that comes is almost always a paddle battle, which means multiple people battling for one wave. I decide to let them battle it out and play it down. A few more roll by and then comes my wave. As it slowly builds, I paddle into it at just the right time and pop up easily.

Once I'm up, I clear my head and just go for it. I kick it off with a vertical backhand snap, following with a bit of clidro and a slob air reverse, showing off by pulling the board in close to me and kick the tail down a bit, like I would on my snowboard. I hit the water smoothly and with Sawyer's "junkyard dog" comments in mind, show off just a bit more by performing a perfect 360° shove-it, turning the board all the way around beneath my feet. I finish with a kickout, which is when a surfer ends a ride by riding over the top of the wave. I bail and start paddling out to the lineup again.

Remembering what Papaw said, I wait patiently for another wave. Then I see it. Being just slightly ahead of the other girl trying to ride it, I paddle in and pop first and from then on, it's my wave. I even hit it so well timed and placed that I drop back into a perfect curl for a nice tube ride, which should earn me extra points. This time, I piece together a 360° carve, a big slob air reverse, and a layback, adding a slash at the end and shooting up loads of spray. At this point, I've probably secured my spot. Deliver a third wave like that and I'm sitting pretty for semi finals.

And deliver, I do. The next two waves are of equal or maybe even better than the first two. After that, I sit back and let the other girls go for their waves, but if a good one comes, I go for it just for fun (and to rub it in Sawyer's face). We all head in at the horn and I'm now sitting in first place going into semi finals. "I told you, that slob air reverse is your best play, with the layback close second," Papaw says. "Use them when you can, because they can turn an average wave into a winning score."

"Got it," I assure him. Grammy gets the semi-final heat sheet. This time, the first heat is Kara, Paige, McKayla, Sally and I.

After the long beep of the horn, I pull ten fantastic waves, including the slob air reverse in half of them and laybacks in almost all of them. Mac catches one particularly sick air and few other stellar waves, but the other girls have also upped their game. When we get out of the water, though, it appears they haven't stepped it up enough. I'm still in the top spot. McKayla's amazing air showed in her score, pushing her up to second, above Sally. She shoots me that competitively devilish smile and I smirk at her. Sorry, Mac. Love ya, but if this goes as planned, I'll be the winner, bar none.

The next two heats are basically useless and tell us what we already know, which is Mac, Kara, Paige, Sally & I are the top surfers. Minutes later, we're back in the water. Within my first two waves, Sally has cut me off, and Paige should've been disqualified for trying to knock me off my board. This just confirms my suspicion: they don't think they can beat me without sabotaging me. Believe it or not, this is good. You know, as long as I don't get sabotaged on more than seven waves.

Sally gets pummeled by the next wave after losing her footing and eventually, Kara goes down too. They both recover quickly, though. I squeeze in two good waves, but the score I need relies on my last scoring ride. Alright, that's it. I don't know how to actually say a hail-Mary, but if I did, I'd be saying one right now. I'm going for the Stalefish air reverse. Am I crazy? Undoubtedly. Is it risky? Yeah, you might say that. Will it win me first place and bragging rights to Sawyer if I do it right? Absolutely.

Let's do this.

I wait for the right wave and a minute later, it comes. I ride in with perfect timing and pop as quick as I can. My bottom turn is flawless and sets me in good positioning. I start off with a 360° carve and a big slash off the top. I swerve down, get a little clidro going, then go for the jump. The second my board leaves the wave, I grab the back side with my left hand and spin as fast as I can. I'm too high off the wave to land at 180°, so I go for the full 360° rotation and land smoothly. With a layback to cap it off, I kick out and jump off the board. As I paddle back out to the lineup, Mac stares at me, open-mouthed.

"Tell me that was not a Stalefish air reverse," she says. "You've only been practicing it for a week! How is it possible that you just perfectly executed a Stalefish air with 360° rotation?"

"I've been practicing that a lot longer than a week," I reply. "That move won me at least two snowboard competitions."

"Unbelievable. I'm best friends with the girl equivalent of Kelly Slater!" she exclaims. Kelly Slater is an eleven-time ASP (Association of Surfing Professionals) World Tour champion.

"I'm not the girl equivalent of Kelly Slater," I laugh. "Just a snowboarder in a different kind of snow."

"Okay, fine. The female version of Shawn White. Happy?" she corrects. I laugh and roll my eyes, paddling into the next wave. Just because I'm excited that I can, I pull two more waves with Stalefish airs. From there, I kick back and let the others duke it out, which they do until time is up. I'm receiving dirty looks from everyone but

McKayla in the water, but on the shore, everyone's rushing for me. Thankfully, Papaw gets to me first.

"That was fantastic. I'm so proud of you," he says, putting an arm around my wet shoulders. I grin, ecstatic. The only thing that could make me more excited is what comes next.

"The 15-18 girls division winners are: In third place, McKayla Atwood," a woman's voice announces over the loud speaker. "In second place, Paige LeGroe; and in first place, Andrea Maverick." Papaw squeezes my shoulders as I laugh with glee and turn towards Grammy, who envelopes me in a hug immediately.

"The 15-18 boys division winners are:" the loud speaker woman begins again. "In third place, Jonathan Stacey; in second place, David Bowen; and in first place, Sawyer Hensley." I glimpse Sawyer slapping high fives with his friends and he shoots me a warm smile and a shaka. I grin and shoot one back, feeling either gracious or delirious after my win.

"Andrea! How did you pull off that Stalefish air?" a reporter shouts a few feet away in the crowd.

"Lots of practice on different terrain," I reply. He writes something down on his notepad, then heads over to Sawyer.

The girls 17-18s go about the same way. I'm on fire today! I pull slob airs and Stalefish airs left and right, dominating the division. A few hours later, I'm announced as first place of the 17-18s as well.

Since we have to stick around for the awards, Mac and I pull off our rash guards and throw on our shorts. Instead of a t-shirt, today I brought my favorite multicolor woven pullover. I roll up the sleeves and pick a spot in the front of the crowd to watch Sawyer, because when I can't hear him annoying me, I can kind of enjoy watching him surf. He's an exceptional surfer, but I would never tell him that. Sitting in the sand with my knees pulled into my chest, I feel relaxed and happy. And tired. Scratch that, exhausted. Just give me my trophies and let me go home to bed.

A few hours later, they do. A crowd gathers around the podium and they present the 15-18 girls awards first, then the boys. The six champions stand side by side as they hand out the trophies. I shake hands with each of the girls and Sawyer does the same with the boys, then extends his hand to me as well. I smile and shake his hand. "So, junkyard dog may have been a little off," he admits.

"You're not such a shubie yourself," I reply. He grins. I like the way his smile lights up his eyes.

After that, they go through the 15-16s and then the 17-18s. Now that I have two gold and blue Junior Championships trophies in hands, my job here is done.

At home, I snap a photo of the trophies and post it on Twitter, captioned "Two new additions to the collection :) #JuniorChamp #2in1day" Immediately, Amy replies, even though it's almost two in the morning in New York and her camping trip is over.

"Congrats girl! Miss you!" she says with a little emoji face blowing me a kiss. I smile and switch to the phone app, tapping in my mother's phone number.

"You've reached Charlotte Maverick. Please leave me a message with your name and phone number and I'll get back to you as soon as I can."

"Hi mom, it's me. Just wanted to tell you I won both of my divisions today at junior champs," I inform the recorder. "Call me when you get the chance."

I hang up and call my dad. "This is Sean Maverick. Leave me a message and I'll get back to you soon." The beep sounds .

"Hi Dad. I just called to tell you I won my divisions at junior championships today and I love you. Talk to you later." I sigh, turn off my phone and set the trophies on the shelf, then crawl into bed and drift off.

TEN

"Come on! Please! I never get to do anyone else's hair!" whines McKayla.

I roll my eyes and take my hair out of it's french braid, letting it fall around my shoulders. I stare at it in her bedroom mirror and finally respond: "Whatever." I try to hid a smile, but it gets out before I can stop it.

"Yes!" she exclaims. She cranks up the volume on her laptop, blasting her music all around the room. Within minutes, her white vanity is covered in all kinds of bottles, brushes and tools. She pulls up a Pinterest board on her laptop and starts looking for a hairstyle for me. "Okay, do you want Victoria's Secret Angel curls, this waterfall braid or…" She trails off, still scrolling.

"I want nothing to do with anything that has Victoria's Secret in front of it," I state.

"Ooooh!" she squeals. "We're doing this one!" She points to an elaborate curly undo with a white rose pinned in it. "I even have a rose clip like that."

"That looks like a bridal hair do," I protest.

"It is, but it's gorgeous! And it's not like we can't simplify it for tonight," she fights back. I groan and she claps. "Yay!"

The "simplified" version of this complicated updo takes the next three-and-a-half hours. First, she curls my entire head of hair, which alone takes ages. Then, she carefully pins the curls up into elegant sections, creating one big curly updo at the nape of my neck. After expertly placing a few small curls around my face, Mac pins in a fake off-white rose, which I have to say, gives it the perfect touch. I still say it looks way too formal for a plain old campfire, but I can't hide the fact that I like it.

Given that we only have a half an hour left, Mac settles on letting me french braid her hair like Elsa from *Frozen*. The only real difference between a french braid and an Elsa braid is that with an Elsa braid, you tease it like crazy.

"Now, for outfits," she says. "Wear the blouse Grammy made you. The hand-painted silk one. Pair it up with off-white bottoms and your gold sandals."

I salute her. "Yes, ma'am!"

We give each other one final hair check, then slip on our shoes and I run across the street to my house. "Andrea!" Grammy calls.

"Hang on!" I call. I pull the light pink blouse McKayla instructed me to use out of my closet apprehensively. Examining it, I sigh. "It's not like I'm going in the water," I say to myself. The hand-painted off-white flowers and delicate material can't be washed, so salt water obviously would not be a good idea. I slip on the cool silk blouse over my light pink tank top and throw on a pair of off-white, high waisted shorts. I tuck the silk in carefully, situating the collar and ruffles delicately. I grab my favorite guitar in it's sticker-covered case from my room and head back out to the living room.

"What's up?" I inquire.

"Your hair is so cute!" Grammy compliments. I laugh.

"McKayla insisted. I said it looked like something for a wedding, but you know McKayla," I inform her. I follow her outside and hop in the car, waving at Mac and her family. "See you there!"

"See you there!" she calls back.

A few minutes later, I jump out into the sand, guitar case still in tow. I spot a cluster of people on the beach, huddled around a soft glow. The sky is lit up over the water with the most brilliant shades of orange, red, pink and purple, reflecting on the crystal clear surface of the sea. "Andrea! Wait up!" McKayla calls from behind me.

"Go faster, Gidget!" I return. I spot Michael by the fire. "Come on, your boyfriend's waiting!"

"You know, not all of us have perfect long ballerina legs!" I laugh and slow down a little bit. "How are you doing this with a huge guitar case in your hand?"

"A lot of practice, Mac," I reply, adjusting my fingers on the black leather handle in my right hand.

McKayla and I are headed to one of the many beach bonfires the Emersons host over the course of the summer. Regardless of how much Sally hates me, her family is nice, and these bonfires are what Oahu teenagers do in place of when Mainlanders go to parties with their friends. I've only ever been to one party and it wasn't nearly as fun as even five minutes at an Emerson bonfire.

"Hey, there you are," Michael greets his girlfriend, slipping his hand into McKayla's when we reach the fire. "Hey Annie."

"Hey Michael," I reply. Michael was one of the neighborhood kids Mac and I grew up playing with, so I'm not surprised he asked Mac out. He was the one who put up with being our knight in shining armor when we played princess and had to be either the dad or the dog every time we played house.

Standing around the campfire is a group of kids that, when in the water (and sometimes out), hate each other, but right now are laughing and joking together. Kara Vanderbilt is chatting with Paige LeGroe and Sally, next to some other kids from around the island and the surfing community. Suddenly, I feel a light tap on my shoulder. Turning around, I see Julia Hensley. I smile.

"Hey Julia," I greet. "What's up?"

"Can you sign this for me?" she asks, holding out a notebook and permanent marker. I laugh, surprised.

"Of course, but I really don't know why you would want my autograph," I reply, taking the notebook from her. I write: *To Julia, the coolest sister anyone could ask for. I wish I had a sister like you :) Keep surfing! Love, Andrea.*

"My brothers say you're gonna be a pro surfer someday," she explains as I write. I hand back the notebook and cast a glance at Sawyer, who's laughing with his brother.

"Well, then, you'd better get your brother's autograph, too," I tell her. "He just as good as me, maybe better." She gives a soft giggle and says a quick "Thank you" before running off to her friends. I laugh as Sawyer and Daniel join us at the fireside.

"What's so funny?" Sawyer inquires.

"You," I answer. I laugh again at his puzzled expression. "Apparently you two think I'm going to be a pro surfer someday and convinced your sister she needs my autograph." He and Daniel laugh.

"What'd you say?" he inquires. I glance at him, wondering if I should tell him what I really said.

"I told her she should get your autograph, too," I reply honestly. "If she's collecting future pro surfer's autographs, she'll need yours in the set." He looks at me, intrigued. "What?"

"I thought you didn't like me," he says, still furrowing his brow at me.

"I don't," I answer, turning my face back towards the fire. "But even pro surfers acknowledge their opponent's skill level. I'd be stupid not to think you a good surfer, regardless of what I think of you out of the water." I turn back to him for a second. "Besides, you told her you thought I was good enough to go pro. I was just being honest." I turn back to the fire, but suddenly I feel hot, and it's not because of the massive cluster of flames in front of me. Sawyer's breath warms the right side of my face and the heat rises in my cheeks. I'm glad it's getting darker quickly.

"So was I," he whispers, making me blush harder in spite of myself. I'm still blushing, but my cheek feels cold when he straightens up and faces the bonfire again.

"Annie, get your guitar!" McKayla calls. A couple other people cheer and I roll my eyes. I open up the big, black, sticker-covered hardshell case. Every time I go to a concert or travel somewhere, I get a sticker and add it to my guitar case. My favorites are the Taylor Swift RED tour sticker, the Sting "Bring On the Night" tour sticker that took me months to find and the large OAHU sticker right in the center.

"Alright, what do you want to hear?" I call.

"Play us some Taylor Swift," Mac replies. I start to pick the strings and sing.

"The way you move is like a full-on rainstorm, and I'm a house of cards. You're the kind of reckless that should send me running, but I kinda know that I won't get far," I sing. "And you stood there in front of me just close enough to touch. Close enough to hope you couldn't see what I was thinking of."

After “Sparks Fly,” the requests keep coming, so I keep playing. I play until they break out the marshmallows and switch out the guitar for a s’more with two chunks of chocolate and two marshmallows between the graham crackers, the way I’ve always done it. The marshmallow’s insides burst and spill out of the little sandwich, coating my fingers in goo. Sawyer, who is now standing behind me, flings his hand out to emphasize his point that the Eric Clapton concert he went to was amazing (which I don’t doubt is true) and accidentally whacks the back of my head, covering it in sweet stickiness. “Oh, gosh, I’m really sorry,” he apologizes. He tries to remove his fingers from my hair. I cry out sharply as he keeps tugging every way he can. “Holy hair product, Batman, what the heck do you have in here? Rubber cement?”

“McKayla!” I shout. Her eyes widen at the situation. “Can you help?”

“I can try,” she replies. I feel her fingers working to untangle his gooey hand from my long, curled strands of hair. After what feels like an eternity, she finally announces she’s done. “As far as your hair goes, the only thing that can help with that is a shower,” she says.

“Or saltwater,” Sawer says deviously.

“Wha-“ I don’t have time to finish before he picks me up and runs down to the waves. “Sawer! Stop it! Quit it!” My shrieks are suddenly cut off as he drops me in the water. I stand up and walk straight up to Jerkface, soaked to the bone with what I’m sure is a murderous look on my face. “Here’s a tip: when a girl who spends all day in the ocean tells you not to get her wet, there’s probably a reason!" I shout at the top of my voice. I storm past him and to the car, Grammy following close behind. "Holy..." I let out a breath through my closed lips, puffing them up with air to keep from cursing.

"Alright, sweetheart, take the blouse off and we'll see if we can do something about the silk," Grammy consoles. I peel off my wet blouse and tank top, leaving me in only my light pink bra and soaked white shorts. I climb in the old van and pull the rose out of my hair. Thankfully, I find a green *Wicked* sweatshirt of mine on the floor and pull it over my head. I climb back out the trunk of the beater, pulling bobby pins out of my hair. Grammy takes the beater and pulls away, going to try and salvage something out of it. I make my way back to the fire, sitting down in one of the beach chairs beside McKayla.

"Are you okay?" she inquires. I huff.

"Yeah, I'm fine. Your gorgeous hairstyle and my shirt aren't, though," I reply bitterly.

"Hey, Andrea!" Sally's brother, Kyle calls. "We need some more entertainment!" I put on a smile and grab my guitar.

"Any requests?" I ask.

"We've given you requests all night," Mac interjects. "Play us something you like." I slide my capo up to the fourth fret of my guitar and slowly begin to strum "The Only Exception" by Paramore.

"When I was younger, I saw my daddy cry and curse at the wind," I sing. "He broke his own heart and I watched as he tried to reassemble it. And my mama swore that she would never let herself forget, and that was the day that I promised I'd never sing of love if it does not exist, but darling, you are the only exception." The lyrics float around my mind as I sing one of my favorite songs.

The song is about a girl like me, a girl who's seen too many hearts break and doesn't believe love exists, finding someone who's the exception to the world's lack of love towards her. When I first heard it, I loved it. It's just... It's me. It's as if I wrote it. I guess I'd be lying if I said I never thought about finding an exception to the world's lack of love towards me. I just know there isn't one. I don't get an exception. And in the long run, that's better for me. It might hurt for a minute or two here and there, but it keeps me from hurting twenty four hours a day, seven days a week.

After a few more songs, someone taps me on the shoulder. Turning around, my eyes meet striking blue ones. "Hey," Sawyer greets softly. "Sorry about earlier. Your grandma told me about your shirt."

"It's okay. It's only a shirt," I brush off, clasping the locks on my guitar case. I stand up and start making the trek to the car.

"A really special shirt that I almost ruined," he corrects. "Sorry about the marshmallow in your hair, too. I only threw you in the ocean just because I thought it'd be funny."

"Hey," I say. "It really is okay. It's just a shirt. Even if it is Chinese silk my mom got me and I hand painted, it's still just a shirt. I'm sorry I blew up at you. I don't have the greatest track record of keeping my temper."

"It's cool. I kind of deserved it," he replies with a small smile. I give him a little smile in return and climb in the car. "See you later."

"See you," I agree. I sigh and put my head up against the trunk of the van as I sit on the rear fender. McKayla comes over and sits down beside me. "That's the last time I let you talk me into letting you give me a makeover."

McKayla laughs. "You always say that and you always end up doing exactly what you said you wouldn't do. I'll get my way eventually."

ELEVEN

"He what?" I ask my grandmother, shocked.

"He invited you to his birthday party," Grammy repeats. "It's nothing big, just a group of kids going to his house and hanging out. They'll be watching a movie. I think Melissa said it's *Divergent*. Mac and Michael will be there, and so will Sally, Kara, Paige, Lexi and bunches of others."

Since it's been a while, I'll bring you up to speed. It's now July 12th, and I am the reigning under eighteen women's Pipeline champion as well as Junior champ. Almost all of my time between Junior Champs and Pipeline has been taken up by training, so I haven't seen Sawyer much, except of course at Pipeline two days ago. Pipeline went fantastically, but now I am faced with a challenge that seems even bigger than taking on the famous (and deadly) waves of Banzai Pipeline: Sawyer Hensley's 18th birthday party.

"Why the heck would he want me at his birthday party? Me, of all people?" I wonder aloud.

"Because you make a good team," she replies. I look at her like she's grown a few extra heads.

"In the words of Bruce Banner, 'we're not a team. We're a chemical mixture that creates chaos. We're a time bomb,'" I quote. Something you may not know about me is I'm multilingual. I speak English, sarcasm, whale, song lyrics and movie quotes. That's one of my favorite moments in *The Avengers.* It's a very accurate description of Sawyer and I, don't you think?

"You seemed to push each other pretty hard at Junior Champs and Pipeline with your smack talk," she says, raising an eyebrow.

"What about the bonfire?" I retort.

"He apologized for that. You made up and you're okay now. Come on, it will be fun."

"Nope. Not gonna do it," I reply, folding my arms like a pouty little kid.

"Annie," she scolds gently.

"I don't want to go."

"Andrea Kalani Maverick, that boy has done nothing to deserve the way you treat him. The incident with your eye was a month and a half ago and it was an accident. He might've smack talked you, but you and McKayla smack talk all the time. McKayla threw paint filled water balloons at your favorite jeans once and you forgave her. All I'm asking is that you make an effort to be nice and start over," she requests. I close my eyes and take a deep breath.

"Fine, I'll go," I reply. "What am I supposed to wear? Sweat-pants? A dress?"

"They said they'll have snacks and hang out first, then watch the movie," she says. "Melissa said she's making her boys dress nicely, so I expect you to do the same. Party starts in an hour. Make an effort!" I get up and go back to my room, wondering how that's supposed to help me choose what to wear.

It's not that I just hate Sawyer. First of all, we've barely even spoken since the campfire. Second of all, I'm just not a party person. I don't like being in big groups of people most of the time. The Emersons' campfires are the closest I get to parties. I know, it doesn't seem like it, but I would much rather sit and read of book than go and watch a movie with a bunch of kids who are going to talk through the whole thing. A cup of tea, some Nutella and a good novel definitely sounds better than pizza, pop and a group movie to me.

After several minutes of staring at my closet and getting no where, I resolve to call Mac, who answers immediately. "What are you wearing to this stupid thing?" I ask.

"I'm wearing a short purple dress over crop leggings," she replies. "It's a pretty casual dress though."

"Okay, I need help. Can you come?" I inquire, flopping back on my bed in defeat.

"Be there in 2."

Precisely two minutes later, Mac is searching through my closet, unable to help but marvel at my clothing. I tried to bring only casual stuff, but even that is high fashion, name brand stuff my mom and dad bought me. She seen it before, but even I marvel at it sometimes. Most people never even see brands I own in person. Amy still goes crazy when I let her in my closet back in New York.

"What about this?" she asks, holding up a white Forever 21 dress. It's one of the few dresses I own that I like, mostly because it's more like a tank top with a skirt than a froufy dress. "You look fantastic in white and always have."

"We're watching a movie. You can't kick back and watch a movie in a dress," I counter.

"Deal with it," she says, throwing the dress at me, along with a pair of white lace leggings that come down just below my knees. She gasps suddenly. "You're wearing these too!" she demands, pulling out a box of stiletto Christian Louboutin pumps. They're slingback peep toes with a white background and have splotches of bright colors that look like they were painted on with delicate brush strokes.

"Uh, no. I'm not wearing thousand dollar stilts to a birthday party," I reject, even though the price is not my problem.

"Please? Your grandma said make an effort," she cajoles. I give her the look of death for a few seconds, but when she sets her hand on her hip and stares right back, I concede.

"Fine," I grumble, taking the shoes and dress from her. "These will make me almost as tall as him."

"Just put it on!" she bids. I go into the bathroom next to my room and change. I slide the stretchy white fabric over my head and stick my arms through the holes, then add the leggings. I slide my feet into the shoes and examine myself in the full-length mirror on the door. It's definitely an effort, and I actually am almost as tall as him in these. The leggings are open lace, so they aren't really any warmer than bare legs. The dress skirt comes down just below my fingertips and the waist is about two inches below the bottom of my rib cage. The slim tank top structure of the top shows off my toned and tan arms. It looks good.

"Okay, one more thing," McKayla prompts when I reenter the room. I raise an eyebrow and she pulls out my cosmetics.

"No," I state firmly.

"Yes," she argues. "Just a little."

"I hate you," I grumble as she digs through my makeup bag, extracting foundation and powders and every other makeup known to man. I sit on the end of my bed and let her cover me in makeup.

"Just a little" ends up being an entire makeover including a smoky eye that, I have to admit, looks really good. My bright red lipstick stands out luminously. As a finishing touch (or the final push towards insanity), Mac hands me the Christian Louboutin bow clutch that matches my shoes. I don't bother to argue, I just take it and stick my phone and lipstick in it, even though I'd much rather have my hobo bag.

After everything else is done, I brush out my hair and leave it down for once. It's wavy from being in the french braid almost 24/7, but it looks good. I slip on the shoes, which, even if they are tall, are at least soft thanks to the silky fabric. Standing up, I give myself the once-over in the mirror on my closet door. With the makeup, it's no longer just effort. I am suddenly a striking young woman who can make heads turn without even trying. My dark brown eyes stand out, and my cheeks have just the right touch of color to them to give them definition. I also look like I'm headed out for Fashion Week. Oh, well. Grammy wanted effort. She can deal with this I suppose.

She does more than deal with it, actually. "Oh, Andrea," Grammy sighs as I enter the living room. "You look beautiful."

"Absolutely stunning," McKayla agrees. She's changed into her own purple tunic, a light lavender garment with cap sleeves and a lace overlay everywhere but the sleeves, paired with floral leggings that go down just below her knees. Just then, Papaw walks in. He whistles.

"Where are you girls headed?" he interrogates.

"Sawyer's birthday party," I reply.

"Well, don't get near me with that white dress," he cautions. "I don't want to get you all messy."

"Believe me, I'd love it if motor oil got on this dress right now," I tell him.

"Andrea! Effort!" Grammy repeats.

What I say: "Sorry, got it, effort." What I mean: "Sorry (not sorry)."

"Good," Grammy says, nodding. "In the car, both of you."

The drive is only about ten minutes to his house, which is a decently-sized victorian with the garage on the right side. The driveway and street are both full of cars, so we park a bit down the road and walk up to the door. Mrs. Hensley answers it and smiles. "Look at you girls! McKayla, Michael is in the kitchen waiting for you," she says, waving us in. Mac heads into the kitchen and I linger for a moment in the large, high-ceiling entryway. "Andrea, you look gorgeous." I grin, unable to help myself. Mrs. Hensley is kind of impossible not to like.

"Thank you," I reply. "Your house is amazing."

"We like it," she agrees, nodding, then she turns back to greet more guests. I slowly venture down the hall in what I think is the direction of the kitchen.

I discover I am correct as I enter the room, lined with white cabinets and stainless steel appliances. It's neat and big, but very cozy as well. My eyes travel around the room, taking in who is here until they land on Sawyer. His gaze is fixated on me from his spot across the room. He pulls at the red polo he's wearing and smiles, making his way towards me. I take a few steps closer, but it only takes him a few strides to cross the space between us.

"Andrea," he greets breathlessly. "You look… wow, you look amazing." A light giggle comes out of me, from where, I have no idea.

"Thanks," I say. "You're not so bad yourself."

"Thanks. My mum told me to wear something nicer than a t-shirt," he laughs. I laugh, too.

"Ditto. My grandma and McKayla both kept telling me to make an effort."

"Well, it looks to me like you made a huge effort," he compliments. "I don't think I've ever seen you with your hair down before. Well, down and dry."

"I don't wear it down very often," I explain.

"You should," he recommends. "It's nice." I giggle again and glance down shyly. This girl is not me. I don't know who she is, but it's not me. This girl is gorgeous and giggly and getting along with Sawyer Jerkface Hensley. Although, he seems to be different, too in a way. "Do you want to head outside?"

"Sure," I answer, smiling.

We exit through the sliding door in between the kitchen and living room and into the yard. The backyard is large and filled with people, most of whom I recognize from when I lived here or surf competitions, a few of whom wave or say hi.

In the corner of the yard to my right as I exit through the back door, a PVC rectangle with a white sheet strapped over the edges stands erect just off the patio, with a projector sitting on an old table about twenty feet back. Just after the table, the yard begins to incline up to a lovely little garden that I'm guessing is Mrs. Hensley's. On the hill, blankets and pillows cover the lawn.

To my left on the patio is a table, overshadowed by an umbrella. Various candies, popcorn and other snacks are scattered across the table, with two blue coolers underneath for drinks. "Want something?" Sawyer inquires, noticing me looking at the spread.

"Actually, water would be great," I respond. He reaches into the cooler and retrieves a water bottle for me and a Mountain Dew for himself.

"This seems to be our most common way of getting along," he comments, smiling and handing me the water.

"What?" I ask, puzzled.

"Going to a movie," he clarifies.

"Oh, yeah," I laugh. "So was *Divergent* your choice or…"

"My choice," he replies. "I figured everyone's already seen *Catching Fire* a hundred times, and *Divergent* is another of the few movies I've seen that I've actually read the book of."

"How far did you get?" I inquire.

"I read the whole trilogy and I really don't know why I didn't quit in the first two chapters of *Insurgent*," Sawyer says honestly.

"I quit about halfway through *Insurgent* and made my friend who read the whole thing tell me what happened. Suffice it to say, I was glad I stopped."

"I think *Insurgent* will be better as a movie, but the first one was better as a book," he estimates.

"Same," I agree. "It helps to have Theo James and Shaliene Woodley as your lead love interests."

"They are good," he says, nodding.

"Hi Sawyer," giggles Sally from behind him. He rolls his eyes at me and makes a face, turning around towards her. I stifle my own giggles, biting my lip.

"Hey, Sally, nice to see you," he greets.

"Oh, Annie, you look nice," she compliments in her high-pitched voice, sweeter than the entire layout of candy next to her.

"Thanks, so do you," I say, fighting to keep my voice steady as Sawyer makes more faces at me.

"Something the matter?" she inquires as my laughter bursts forth from me.

"Yeah," I answer, still laughing. "He's an idiot." I shove Sawyer's shoulder playfully. He wears a smug smile for a moment, and then I gasp as he picks me up and throws me over his shoulder, spinning me around. I scream and laugh. "Put me down!" I shout.

"Not until you say I'm totally awesome and not an idiot!" he retorts.

"Fine! You're totally awesome and not an idiot!" I say. He throws me down on a stack of pillows. "Thanks Jerkface," I joke.

"You're welcome, Madame Banshee," he replies, feigning a british accent and giving a little bow, before collapsing next to me. "I think you broke my eardrums."

"Ha, ha," I say sarcastically. "I'm not that loud."

Sally seems to stick to Sawyer like pine tree sap, joining us seconds later. McKayla also has emerged from the house with Michael to join us in the grass. "You wouldn't last a minute in Dauntless," he says, referring to a group of characters in *Divergent*, who, since they value bravery above all else, do crazy and dangerous things to prove their bravery every day. "You were screaming like a crazy person."

"I would too!" I counter. "I'm totally dauntless."

"Prove it," Sally interjects, flicking her eyebrows up in innocent question.

"How?" I ask.

"Walk the top of the garage," she dares. "Or if you're too chicken…"

"I didn't say anything, Sally," I retort. McKayla gives me a look that says "You're really even considering this?"

Standing, I take my shoes off and hand them along with my clutch and water to Sawyer. "Can you hold these for me?"

"Annie, don't be stupid," he says. I huff and put my things down on the blanket instead. I turn towards the garage, but he catches my hand.

"I'm not," I promise. His bright blue eyes are full of worry and maybe even a dash of panic, both of which surprise me.

"Just," he begins. "Just be careful." I nod and squeeze his hand to reassure him.

There's a ladder on the side of the garage that I scale quickly without trouble. Sally has a smug look on her face as I stand and wobble on the metal ridgepole. My bare feet grip the hot metal. It's only a few inches wide and rounded, so it's not easy. I walk forward carefully, going heel to toe. Suddenly, I am at the end and relief floods through me. That wasn't so hard.

"Bring the ladder to the side," I call down. Sawyer moves to help me, but Sally holds him back.

"Walk back," Sally counters. I roll my eyes.

"Sally, no-" Sawyer begins.

"Don't you think she's brave enough to do it?" Sally asks him.

Well, I guess it can't be that much harder than last time. I step carefully and it's going well, when suddenly, a few steps from the edge, I twist my left foot a little bit and a quick, sharp pain shoots up and down it from my knee. I lose my balance and fall forward off the roof, hitting my bad knee on the edge and feeling a piercing pain a hundred times worse than the one a few seconds ago. I hear Sawyer cry my name, but it sounds much further away than he is. I can still catch the desperation in his voice, though. A strangled noise I didn't think I would ever hear, let alone feel come from my own throat, escapes me. I hit the ground and am a little dazed for a minute and my vision is slightly fuzzy. My entire left leg is full of shooting pain that would be enough to make anyone shriek, but for some reason, nothing but heavy breathing comes forth. I can only form one coherent thought, and even that's a little woozy: Thanks, Sally. Thanks a lot.

TWELVE

Unbelievable. Let me get this straight: I've surfed Mavericks (a surf spot where people have died because they wiped out), Pipeline (again, people have died) and taken on surf and snowboard tricks that only pros do without getting hurt, and I just got injured for walking on a stupid garage roof? My mother always said my pride would be my undoing. For some unknown reason, it took me until now to to realize she was right.

"Annie!" Sawyer repeats, dropping to his knees beside me. "Oh, that's not— Daniel get mum! McKayla, call Mrs. Maverick!" He brushes the hair out of my face gently.

"Guess I was a little stupid, huh?" I joke as I try to sit up. I whimper in pain as my knee moves.

"Don't," he commands, laying a hand on my shoulder. "Don't. Just lie still and we'll get you help soon." He takes my right hand in both of his and gently rubs it, and I try to focus on the soft, circular movement of his thumbs to distract me from my knee.

"Sorry I ruined your party," I apologize.

"Don't be," he consoles. "This is a million times more exciting than just watching a movie." I smile a little.

"Sawyer, Daniel told me what happened," Mrs. Hensley says, appearing next to her son.

"Sorry Mrs. Hensley," I say sheepishly.

"Oh, don't apologize, I always knew that Emerson girl was trouble," she replies, pulling out a cell phone and calling 9-1-1. "Yes, hi, I have girl here who was just dared to walk the ridgepole of my garage roof at my son's birthday party, and she fell off and appears to have twisted her knee. Yes, she is conscious. 4589 Clemray Drive. Have you had knee problems before this?" she asks me.

"Chondromalacia in the knee that's twisted," I reply. "No surgery, though." She repeats my answer into the phone and it continues like that for a few minutes. Mac informs me that my grandmother will meet us at the hospital. A few minutes after she hangs up, I hear sirens headed our way. A first response team somehow manages to stabilize my knee as much as they can before they lift me up and put me on a gurney, wheeling me out to the ambulance. Sawyer keeps hold of my hand the whole way. I'm beyond grateful for the support.

"I don't know if I'll be back, just keep everyone calm. Turn on the movie and I'll call when I know about all this," Sawyer tells Daniel. "I'll see you at the hospital, okay?" he tells me. I want to protest and tell him to stay at his party, but all I can to is nod as they lift me into the ambulance. McKayla, Mrs. Hensley and Sawyer get in the truck parked in the driveway and they shut the doors to the ambulance.

Everyone on the first response team starts to ask me questions and I answer them as best I can, but thankfully, it's a very short trip to the hospital. Upon arrival, the team rolls me out and through a series of hallways into a room. "Your family is coming, okay?" a nurse says as I lay there.

"What for?" I ask. Before she can explain, my grandparents enter the room, with Sawyer and McKayla behind them.

"Family only," the nurse demands. I get the feeling she says this a thousand times a day with the trained look she gives my friends.

"No," I interject. "I need them too." She looks at me and glances at my knee.

"Fine, but only for a few minutes," she informs. Sawyer and Mac rush to my side. Sawyer casually slips his hand into mine again and I smile slightly at him and mouth "Thank you." He nods in response and gives my hand a squeeze.

"Mr. and Mrs. Maverick, your granddaughter's knee has been severely dislocated and there appears to be something wrong with her cartilage. To properly set it to actually heal and not cause her more pain, we need to do surgery as soon as possible."

"Well, I suppose if that's the way you have to do it," Papaw replies, glancing at me.

"You'll need to sign some papers and choose a method of anesthetics," she adds. "We can either put her to sleep with general anesthesia, or she can stay awake and we can inject her knee with local anesthesia."

"No way," I reply. "I can't be awake."

"Listen to her," Papaw agrees. Grammy and Papaw each give me a kiss, and then follow the nurse out to file paperwork. I've had general anesthesia before and it's disorienting, but not bad enough to make me want to be awake and alert when they cut open my knee. Mac gives me a hug.

"Make sure he's not worrying about me the whole time at his party," I tell Mac.

"I'm not going back," he protests. "I'm staying here until your surgery's over."

"What good would that do? I won't even be awake for hours," I retort. He hesitates.

"Fine," he decides, then he laughs. "Maybe you should stop hanging out with me. I seem to be very hazardous to your health."

"I'll take my chances," I reply, smiling. He follows Mac out of the room, casting me one last glance.

Several hours later, I wake in a different room. My arm is sore from being poked and prodded and, to my dismay, has a needle stuck in it, and my knee, to say the least, is not comfortable, but much better than it was. My arms prickle with goosebumps from the temperature and the thin hospital gown I've changed into doesn't do much to help. My grandparents sit in chairs in opposite corners of the room, with my grandpa at my side watching television on the flatscreen mounted high on the wall and my grandma underneath the TV, reading a book. A vase of the prettiest red roses I've ever seen sits on the table to my right, with a little card sticking out that reads: "Sally's parents banned her from regionals for daring you. I'll come see you soon. Get better, Madame Banshee. Love, Jerkface." I smile and giggle a little bit.

"Hey, you're awake," Grammy greets softly upon hearing me giggle.

"What time is it?" I ask groggily.

"Almost one in the morning," Papaw answers, yawning. He looks just as tired as he sounds.

"You guys can go home and catch some sleep, you know," I tell them.

"We wanted to be here when you woke up," he says.

"Sawyer and his mom and dad came by earlier," Grammy informs me. I smile.

"I noticed," I reply, nodding at the flowers. Grammy smiles.

"He wanted to stay until you woke up too, but his parents made him go home and get some sleep," she says. "The way he looked at you, I don't think he'll be getting any sleep tonight." I feel myself blush. What is it with the blushing this summer? I almost never blush, and I've probably blushed a hundred times since I got here.

"So what's up with the knee?" I ask, changing the subject.

"Set back in the groove and they've added a little bit of cartilage on one side to fix your chondromalacia," Papaw tells me. "As soon as you recover, you should have a perfectly normal knee."

"Which is when?" I inquire, dreading the answer. I can already guess that I'm down and out for regionals.

"They said recovery should be about six weeks, but I'd be careful about surfing. We'll get you trained up, but I don't know about any more competition," Papaw replies.

"So no regionals."

"No regionals. Probably."

"Great," I huff. "Do either of you have my stuff?"

"Sawyer brought your clutch and shoes over," Grammy answers, handing me the clutch. "I washed your dress out with bleach and it will be fine. The leggings, however, are shredded."

"Thanks. That's okay, I never wear them anyway," I reassure her, reaching for my phone. Clicking the power button, I see that my guess was correct. That cheeky boy. My background is a silly selfie of Sawyer and going into my contacts, I don't find a Sawyer Hensley, but someone entered a new contact called "Jerkface." Hm, I wonder who that could be (wink, wink, nudge, nudge).

I tap out a text message to Jerkface's cell phone number. "Just woke up. Text me when you're up. Thanks for the flowers :-)"

"Alright, Kiddo," Papaw says, standing. "You okay here? You're going to be here for three or four days."

"I'll be fine. Go get some sleep," I assure. They both plant kisses on my forehead and leave. A minute or two after they leave, my phone buzzes. "Haven't been able to sleep at all. Can I come see you?"

"Visiting hours are over," I text with a little emoji sticking it's tongue out at him. "I'm going to be here for 3 or 4 days though. You can come see me tomorrow."

"That's not going to help me sleep," he texts, accompanied by a sleeping emoji.

"Would talking to me help?" I ask. He texts back a thumbs-up and my phone starts to ring. I answer immediately. "Hey, Jerkface."

"Hey." His deep voice sounds rough and sleepy.

"Why can't you sleep?"

"I'm…" He hesitates. "I'm worried about you. You freaked me out, you know, falling off the roof and nearly tearing your leg in two."

"For the record, it was already loose and just got knocked out of the joint," I console. "I'm okay, really. Not fond of hospitals or needles, though, both of which I have to deal with right now."

"I feel really bad for not sticking up for you to Sally," he confesses.

"You didn't have to," I reply. "And you did. I was just too cocky to stand up for myself."

"I know, but I should've done more," he combats. A short silence ensues.

"Do you want to come watch a movie tomorrow? Visiting hours open at eight, I think," I inquire. "I have DVD player here in the room."

"Sure. Why don't we pick up where we left off with *Divergent*?" he asks. I smile.

"Of course," I answer. "Get some sleep and I'll see you tomorrow. If I'm asleep, wake me up. Trust me, I won't care."

"Okay," Sawyer says. "Goodnight, Annie."

"Goodnight, Sawyer."

The next morning, my eyes flutter open to meet a pair of familiar brown eyes staring at me. "Morning," I yawn. "You know, I told you you could wake me up."

"I know," Sawyer replies, smiling. "You looked too peaceful. I thought you could use the rest." I smile and feel my cheeks get hot, even though the rest of me is cold. Just then, a nurse enters the room to check my vitals.

"Today, we're going to have a physical therapist come in and help you start rehab," she informs me. "We might take you off the IV pain meds and give you oral meds instead too."

"Okay. How soon could I get the IV out?" I ask anxiously.

"How much pain do you feel right now on a one-to-ten scale, one being no pain, ten being you feel like you're dying?" she asks. I think for a second.

"It's about a two," I reply.

"I'll talk to your doctor. We've been slowly reducing the amount of medication going through the IV all night, so we could take it off you as soon as you're comfortable if he okays it," she says. I nod.

"I don't like needles and I want to wear a sweatshirt," I inform her. "I'd be comfortable taking it out now if I could." She leaves to go get the doctor as my grandparents enter the room.

"Hi Sawyer," Grammy says. "Hey sweetheart. The nurse told us you want to get rid of the IV?"

"A. S. A. P.," I reply. "I can't have a needle stuck in my arm for much longer."

"Okay, darling," she consoles. "The doctor's coming. Don't worry."

"Guess we'd better wait until they're done with all this to watch the movie," he suggests. "You said you're cold?" I nod. "Hang on a minute. I'll be right back." He heads out the door. A second later, it opens again.

"Hey, Andrea, how are you?" the doctor asks upon entering, consulting his clipboard. "How's the knee?"

"It's okay. I'd like to get the needle out of my arm, though," I reply. He nods and asks a few questions while he fiddles with the machine I'm hooked up to.

"Well, I'd say we can take you off this bad boy and let you start taking pain meds orally," he finally announces. "You want me to take it out now?"

"That'd be great," I reply. He turn off the machine and slowly removes the IV needle from my arm, sticking a bandaid on after.

"Just let a nurse know if you need something," he replies, exiting.

"So Sawyer's here," Grammy observes. I nod.

"He came as soon as visiting hours started," I reply with out a doubt. "I texted him last night and he couldn't sleep. He wanted to know I was okay, so I called him and we agreed to watch *Divergent* this morning."

"Oh, okay," Grammy replies, smiling. Sawyer enters before I can ask her why she's looking at me weird.

"Sorry, had to run out to my car for something," he says. Grammy and Papaw smile at him.

"Well, I guess we'll leave you to it," Grammy sighs. "Annie, call us if you need anything. Your parents might call at some point, because we talked to them last night before you woke up."

"Okay," I say, nodding. "Love you."

"Love you too," they reply, heading out.

"You still cold?" Sawyer asks, standing and putting in the DVD in the player. I nod.

"Yes. It's like a freaking meat locker in here," I affirm.

"Here," he says, grabbing a black mass of fabric from the chair he previously occupied. As he unfolds it, I discover it's a sweater, which he helps me put on. It's a big black knit sweater that smells like cologne and a little bit of hair product. The scent is soothing and comforting.

"Thanks," I say. "If the chairs are uncomfortable, I can scoot over if you want."

"Nah, I'm good," he replies, hitting a few buttons on the DVD remote. About five minutes later, he stands up. "Okay, no. I'm not good. These chairs are about as good as rocks for seating. Scoot." I laugh and scoot over, making room for him to sit. It's a little squeezed, so he puts his arm around my shoulders. I snuggle into his shoulder, feeling more relaxed than I have in a long time.

A little later, my phone rings. It's my mom, so Sawyer pauses the movie and decides to go get a soda from the vending machine. He points at me as if asking "you want anything?", to which I say "Dr. Pepper." He nods and leaves as I answer. "Hello?"

"Honey! I was so worried about you! Grammy and Papaw said you fell off a roof and dislocated your knee and had to have surgery and-"

"Mom, I'm okay," I cut her off. "I'm fine. I'm in the hospital watching a movie with a friend. They took the IV out and my knee really doesn't hurt that bad right now."

"Mac?" she inquires.

"No, Mac's coming later I think," I reply. "It's Sawyer, the boy I told you about."

"The one who's an idiot? Or the twenty year old?"

"The one that's my age," I answer.

"Oh, so he's not an idiot any more?" she prods.

"Mom, it's complicated," I reply. Just like the rest of my life.

"Well, have fun sweetheart," she sighs. "I love you."

"I love you, too," I echo. "Bye." I hang up and decide to call my dad, as Sawyer isn't back yet.

"Hello?"

"Hey Dad."

"Hey, sweetheart! What happened? Your grandparents said you fell off a roof?"

"Yeah, I'm okay though," I assure. "Sally Emerson dared me to walk the ridgepole of my friend Sawyer's garage, which I did, then twisted my leg funny at the edge and fell off. I hit my knee on the way down."

"Ouch. Feel better kiddo. At least you got the competitions out of the way before this happened. Let me know if you need anything," he instructs. "I love you."

"Love you too," I echo as Sawyer reenters the room, thinking of regionals. "Bye."

"One Dr. Pepper," he says, handing me the bottle of soda and taking his place beside me, hitting play and placing his arm around me again.

Okay. Maybe he isn't such a jerkface after all.

THIRTEEN

I wake up warm and cozy, still wrapped in Sawyer's arms. I'm not quite sure when I fell asleep, but I must've been more exhausted than I thought. I almost never fall asleep during movies. I yawn and move my head back just slightly to look up at Sawyer. "Hi."

"Hey, you're awake," he says happily. "Mac texted you to see when she could come and I texted her back that she could come when you woke up."

"Thanks," I respond. "And thanks for letting me sleep. I needed that."

"No problem," he replies. "I'd better go. Training for regionals."

"Have fun," I quip. He gets up to leave when I remember the sweater. "Oh, don't forget your sweater."

"Keep it," he says. "I hardly ever wear it anyway, and it looks good on you." I smile, twisting the ends of the too-long sleeves around my hands.

"Thanks," I reply, smiling. He smiles back and leaves.

A few minutes later, McKayla arrives and gives me a hug. She sniffs around me. "That's not your sweater," she states, pulling back and pointing at it. "It wasn't in your closet yesterday and it smells like cologne. Who's is it?"

"Oh, it's Sawyer's," I tell her. "I was cold earlier and he went out to get this from his car for me." She laughs and makes the face that reminds me of the one she made when she wouldn't tell me what she was giggling about at Junior Champs. "What?" I demand. "What are you so crazy about?"

"Can't you see it?" she inquires. "You and Sawyer."

"What about Sawyer and I?" I ask.

"You like each other!" she exclaims.

"What?! I don't like him, not like that!" I defend.

"Well, he likes you," she comes back. She sits down on the edge of the bed. "You can't tell me you don't like him."

"I don't!" I repeat.

"Unbelievable," she laughs. "He's your very own, real life Mr. Darcy and you don't even know it." I open my mouth to retort but nothing comes out.

We move on and have a fun time hanging out together, but I can't get what she said off my mind. I still can't get it off my mind three days later when I've been released from the hospital. My grandmother stands at the kitchen counter making sourdough bread, having just watched *Pride and Prejudice* again with me. I sit at the kitchen table with my leg propped up on a few chairs and wrapped in ice, twisting the sleeves of Sawyer's black sweater around my hands, pondering whether to ask my grandmother about it or not.

"Grammy?"

"Yes, sweetheart?" she replies, glancing up from her dough.

"Do you think anyone would ever fall in love with me?" I say tentatively. "Regardless of whether I wanted to fall in love or not."

"Oh, most definitely," she responds confidently.

"Why do you think so?" I inquire.

"My darling, you underestimate yourself. You are beautiful, kind, loving, sweet, smart and a good friend. You're just the kind of girl a boy would fall head over heels for." Her eyes flick down at my sweater and smiles as if she knows who I have in mind. I heave a sigh.

"I told McKayla I don't like him, but I don't know," I say, looking down at my sleeves. "I don't know how I feel about him. I like having him as a friend, and I like the feeling of being around him. I like…" Things keep coming to me, and it seems that now I've begun, I can't stop. I shock myself with how much detail I can go into. I've paid more attention to him than I thought I did. "I like the way he smells, and the way he gets so worried about me, and the little tiny waves in his hair. I like how it feels when I'm wrapped up in his arms. I like playing movie trivia with him and how he's so competitive. I like how much his eyes remind me of the sea. But at the same time, I'm scared."

"Andrea, you don't need to be scared," she advises, smiling. "You need to be cautious. When you aren't careful is when you get hurt. When you are scared, though, it could hurt you even worse. My advice, sweet girl, is to be cautious, but listen to your heart as well as your head."

Two weeks later, I'm standing on crutches on the Hensleys' porch for the eighth time since my knee injury. Sawyer has made it a point to help me not be bored out of my mind, so either he's come over to my house or I've gone over to his house almost every day since I was released. Melissa, as she has told me to call her, opens the door with a smile and helps me in. Sawyer is kneeling down by the large DVD cabinet underneath the TV mounted on the wall and must hear my crutches on the wood floor. "*Spiderman* or *Captain America*?" he inquires.

"Ooh, tough," I say, pondering the choice. I think about it as I situate myself on the couch. "*Spiderman.* I'm in an Andrew Garfield/ Emma Stone kind of mood."

"You read my mind," he agrees, popping the disc in the player and coming to help me get comfortable. He kneels down and pulls the ottoman a little closer for me to prop my feet up on, then helps me finish wrapping an ice pack around the joint and strapping it down with Ace bandages.

Peter Parker becomes Spider Man, falls in love with Gwen Stacey and saves New York City all in two hours and then, instead of engaging me in some debate about the movie as he usually does, we sit in silence. He's reading the back of the DVD case and I have begun playing with the hem of my t-shirt. My eyes have gone out of focus ("staring into space," as my dad would call it).

"How long have you had your board?" Sawyer asks out of the blue.

"The one here? About three years," I reply. "I have a newer longboard at my Dad's house, though." He nods.

"Do you want to make a new one?" he inquires, smiling and eyebrows raised. I look at him quizzically.

We manage to get up and hobble outside. Sawyer leads me inside what looks like a big shed, but upon entering, I discover it's a workshop. It smells like wood and foam and the workbenches that encircle the room are covered in power tools, some typical things like drills and cutters and others like I've never seen before.

He sets a piece of foam with a strip of wood called a stringer running down the middle on the work table beside me and grabs two pairs of goggles, handing one to me. I lean my crutches against the wall and try to work without them, like the doctor told me to start trying to do.

"That's called a blank. It's the foundation of the board," he defines, pointing at the foam. "How long to you want the board to be?"

"5' 10"," I reply. "The one I have is six feet, but I'm used to working a five foot snowboard, so a few inches off might improve it a little."

"Okay, so the first thing we'll do is get a template," he begins, dashing into another room. He returns with a sheet of plywood in the shape of a 5' 10" board and lays the blank down on the wooden workhorse in the center of the room.

After laying the template on top of the blank, he traces the template carefully on both the front and back and cuts the foam. Then, he cuts a thin layer of foam off the deck (the top) to make it smooth, doing the same to the bottom. "Come here," he instructs. He takes my hands in his and wraps my fingers around the handles of the carving tool. "Just gently shave down the blank until you have the rails you want. Like this." He helps me drag the tool across the edges of the board, perfectly curving the edges.

"Now use this to shape the board," he tells me, holding up a piece of steel. "It's a steel mesh. It gives you the smooth, perfect curve you want." He lets me try it by myself for a moment, then trades me and goes to work on it. I love watching him work. He looks like he does in the water: driven and focused, but with the edges of his mouth hinting at a smile. The muscles of his arms stand out as he drags the mesh across the board.

He turns the blank over and shapes the bottom, then lays a cloth over it, trimming and cutting the cloth to fold it over the rails. After the fabric is folded correctly, he has me mix and pour a bucket of resin over both the board and cloth. Quickly, he squeegees the board in an infinity symbol pattern to smooth it out. "It'll have to set for about a day," he says, putting his goggles down and taking mine. "Want to come over again to work on it tomorrow?"

"I'd love to," I reply. "You're really good at that."

"Oh, thanks," he says, smiling. "I started making my own boards with my dad when I was about ten."

"Pretty nice skill to have," I laugh.

"Yeah, it's not bad," he agrees. He retrieves my crutches and carries them back to the house as I try to walk. I stumble a little bit, and he slips his hand into mine, helping me to walk through the house and out front to the Jeep. He helps me in and drives me home.

The next three days, I go over to his house to work on the board. On the fourth and last day of building the board, I decide to skip the crutches all together. Sawyer said to wait until later this afternoon to come over. Around two in the afternoon, Papaw strides into the living room with a triumphant look on his face. "Well, girls, I finally did it," he announces. "I finally fixed up old Gertrude."

"She runs?!" I exclaim. He nods.

"Just took her out for the first time in ten years," he replies. My grandmother rolls her eyes, but smiles in spite of herself.

Gertrude is the bike my grandpa has had forever. Before my grandparents were dating, my grandmother said that bike was his girlfriend. She came up with the name Gertrude and it stuck. Gertrude died when I was eight and Papaw has tried to fix her ever since, even though he has another bike that he actually rides and lets me ride when I'm here. Between training for competition and my knee injury, I haven't taken a ride all summer.

"Want to take her for a spin?" he inquires. My eyes widen as I grin and nod.

"Annie, really? A motorcycle?" Grammy interjects. "Is this really a good idea?"

"Grammy, the therapist said I can ride a bike with my knee," I comfort. "I don't even have to pedal a motorcycle. I'll be fine."

"Alright," she consents, throwing her hands up as if she knows there's nothing she can do about it.

"Let's go!" Papaw cries. I follow him out to the garage and take the helmet he gives me. After putting it on, I heave my right leg over the bike and turn the key. The engine roars to life and Papaw grins. I flip up kickstand and ride down the driveway, zooming around the block. The wind on my face, I feel like I could just keep going forever. Upon pulling back into the driveway, I check my phone. Sawyer has texted me, saying it's okay to come over now.

"Hey, can you take me to Sawyer's?" I ask Papaw.

"Why don't you just take the bike?" he suggests.

"Really?"

"Yeah, you were riding perfectly fine out there." I kiss his cheek and "run" (more like speed walk) into the kitchen to grab my bag.

"I'm going to Sawyer's," I inform Grammy, giving her a kiss on the cheek too.

"Okay, have fun," she replies.

I put my helmet back on and mount the bike again, kicking the kickstand and taking off. About ten minutes later, I pull up in front of Sawyer's house. "So you're a biker girl now, are you?" Sawyer greets, leaning against the doorframe. "I didn't know that." I laugh.

"I've always been a biker girl," I reply with a coy smile. "And you don't know everything about me."

"Come on, your board's dry, we just have to sand it and add the leash," he bids. I follow him out back and follow his instruction in the workshop, sanding the board down and adding a long black leash. An hour or two later, we're done and the board looks fantastic.

"Thank you," I say gratefully. "It's gorgeous."

"No problem. It has to sit for three days, though before you can use it," he replies. "So seriously, when did you get a motorcycle?"

"My grandpa has had that old thing since before he and my grandmother were even dating," I laugh. "However, it died about ten years ago and he got it running today."

"I've always wanted to learn how to ride a motorcycle," he says wistfully.

"Do you want to try?" I inquire, eyebrows raised.

"I don't have a helmet, though," he points out.

"Give me twenty minutes," I reply. I put on my own helmet and race off to my house, grabbing an extra helmet out of the garage and racing back.

"Here," I say, handing him the helmet when I'm back in his driveway. He fastens it on and climbs on the bike behind me, wrapping his arms around my waist. "Where do you want to go?"

"Anywhere."

"Hold on tight."

FOURTEEN

The two of us drive around the island, taking in the scenery, until Sawyer says “here. Stop here.” I pull over to the beach spot he’s point to and park the bike, letting him off first. I swing my leg over, pull my helmet off and shake out my hair.

“Why here?” I inquire curiously as he takes off his backpack. I didn’t notice the bag before: a large, black, L. L. Bean backpack.

"I figured we'd have a little change of scenery for dinner," he answers coyly with a smile. I smile back and roll my eyes.

It turns out, he can do a lot in twenty minutes. He's made two sandwiches, brought a bag of chips, a Dr. Pepper and Mountain Dew. He's also managed to snag a few of his mom's chocolate chip cookies which are quite possibly the closest thing to heaven on earth achievable. I don't know why or how, but they just are.

"So," he begins, once we're seated on the sand and eating our sandwiches. "You're right. I don't know anything about you. I feel like I know nothing about you other than you surf and I know your favorite movies."

"Same. Favorite color, go," I start, taking a sip of my soda.

"Blue," he replies. "You?"

"Teal. When's your birthday?"

"July tenth."

"Mine's August sixteenth. Favorite surf spot?"

"Pipeline."

"Mine's Mavericks," I reply, taking a big bite of my chicken salad sandwich (also a Melissa Hensley creation).

Sawyer pauses, chewing and thinking, then decides "It's because you're absolutely nuts."

"I am not!" I push his shoulder as he laughs.

"What's the one thing you wanted most for Christmas as a kid?" he asks.

"A puppy. Hands down. Still want one, actually. You?"

"I always wanted one of those gigantic automatic Nerf guns. I got it when I was ten," he laughs. "Favorite book?"

"That is like asking a mother to choose her favorite child."

"Fine, top five books or series."

"*Three Hours Too Soon*, *Pride and Prejudice*, the *Harry Potter* series, the *Anne of Green Gables* series and the *Traveler's Gift* and sequel, *The Final Summit*," I finally reply.

"*Three Hours Too Soon, Harry Potter, Hunger Games, The Outsiders,* and I actually really like *To Kill a Mockingbird*. Favorite music artists?"

"Taylor Swift, Carrie Underwood, One Direction, Eric Clapton and Sting. Other than that, it's a lot of different songs by different bands."

"Sting is pretty great," he agrees. "I like the rest of them too. My favorites, though, are U2 and Eric Clapton. Other than that, like you said, a lot of different songs by different bands."

"Like what?"

"Here," he replies, hitting shuffle on his phone. "Tonight Tonight" by Hot Chelle Rae comes on and I laugh.

"You like this song too? My friends tease me all the time for still being into this song," I laugh.

"Heck yeah! It's a good song!" he agrees. He starts to lip-sync along, which makes me laugh even harder. "What I Like About You" comes on next, to which he gets up plays air guitar. To my protesting, he pulls me to my feet and tries to get me to dance. "Please?" he begs, making puppy dog eyes and a pouty lip.

"No, I'm a terrible dancer," I counter.

"And I'm good?!" he exclaims. I roll my eyes and get up for the rest of the song. We laugh and dance ridiculously, lip-syncing and playing air guitar all the while. After it's over, "The Only Exception" by Paramore comes on, making my smile disappear a little. "What's the matter?" Sawyer asks, noticing. "I thought you liked this song."

"Nothing," I reply, smiling again. "And I do." He holds out his hand to me. I was afraid he'd do that.

"May I have this dance?" he inquires. I hesitate, then take his hand. He brings it up and lays it on his shoulder, along with the other and sets his own hands on my waist. My heart rate accelerates to a million miles per minute as he gazes into my eyes.

I laugh nervously. "I've never actually danced with a guy before," I confess.

"Really?" I nod. "I can't imagine why."

"What do you mean?"

"You're amazing." The words make the heat rise in my cheeks.

He continues to stare into my eyes and goes on. "You're beautiful and smart and funny. You've got fantastic taste in movies, music and books." I laugh. "You. Are. Amazing."

"You're not too bad yourself," I laugh. He smiles warmly and stares into my eyes again. Suddenly, he's leaning in closer to me and I realize he's about to kiss me. I take my hands off his shoulders and turn around. "I think we should, um, go."

"Oh." I can't see his face right now, and I'm glad I can't. His voice alone is enough to almost make me cry out of sympathy. "Alright."

I strap on my helmet as he packs up his backpack and mounts the bike behind me. At his house, he gets off without a word. Not even a goodbye. I watch the door shut behind him, then hit the gas and blaze down the street.

I drive home, park the bike and run inside to throw myself on my bed without greeting anyone. I must've slammed the door without noticing, though, because a moment later, I feel the bed sink down beside me and a gentle hand begin to rub my back. A waterfall of silent tears trail down my face. "Grammy," I whimper.

"I'm here, sweetheart."

"Why'd he have to go and do that?" I ask, trying to be angry, but it comes out sad. I shift to face her.

"What did he do?" she asks gently.

"He tried," I sniff. "He tried to kiss me. We were having a fine time until he asked me to dance and then he tried to kiss me!"

"What did you do?"

"I stopped dancing with him and said 'I think we should go.'" She closes her eyes as if pained by this answer. "Why'd he have to ruin it?! We were finally getting along, when he just, he, he had to go and ruin it!"

After a short pause, she answers "Because he loves you."

"What?" I ask, disbelieving, sitting up.

"He loves you," she repeats. I shake my head.

"He can't," I protest.

"He does."

I fold my arms together and sit there, unwilling to believe it.

"Just think about it," Grammy says, laying a black sweater around my shoulders before she leaves.

I pull the sweater off and toss it on the floor, as I am already verging on overheated. About to turn around and go sit outside, I stop short at the sight of the black mass of fabric, all balled up on the ground. I turn around again and pick it up. It's his. The one he gave me at the hospital.

Memories start to flood back to me. He wasn't able to sleep after I got hurt. He was worried about me when Sally dared me. He spent tons of time with me, keeping me from getting bored with my injury. He built me a new board. He danced with me. He tried to kiss me.

He loves me.

FIFTEEN

I change into a black tank top and pull the sweater on overtop, heading outside afterwards. For hours I just sit there, thinking. He loves me. Well, he did. Who knows how he feels about me now?

Why do I even care? It would never last. It could never work. I live on one coast half of the year and the other coast the other half. I'm only here every other holiday. And what if his family decided to move back to Australia? Then we'd have an over fifteen hour time difference to deal with, in addition to the miles between us.

I stand up and slip on my shoes, going out to the garage and grabbing the keys to Gertrude. I just drive, the night wind on my face. I drive until I find a nice little spot to park by the beach and walk around with the sand on my toes. It happens to be the same spot where Sawyer and I were earlier. I don't even really remember how I got here. I just drove until I found it.

As Grammy, Papaw and everyone else on the island except maybe the one person that won't talk to me are asleep, I stare up at the night sky and start to talk to the one person *not* on the island who might listen to me for the first time in a long time. That is, if He's there.

"Hey, God," I begin. I grimace at my own words. I take a deep breath, wondering how to continue. "Look, I'll be honest: I haven't talked to you in forever by myself. I don't really remember how to do it. Anyway, what's up? I know it's all peaches and cream up where you are, but I'm not exactly having the best time down here. You pretty much ditched me about ten years ago, and I'm not even really sure why I'm talking to you, but here I am."

I take a deep breath, feeling anger from the past ten years start to burn inside me. "Why'd you ditch me when I needed you? Everybody says you're loving and all-knowing and all that, but I guess you were too busy to be bothered with a little girl's problems. Seriously? I don't even really think I'm talking to anyone! I'm just shouting into space!" I've started to cry again and I'm glad no one is here to witness my unhinging.

"If you really are there, and you really hear me, help me," I plead. "Give me proof that love exists, not just universally, but for me. Show me that I can actually be loved and I don't need to be scared, like you should have all those years ago. Amen."

I feel a little better after venting, whether some almighty being heard me or not. I twist the ends of Sawyer's sweater around my hands and walk around in the sand, eventually putting my shoes back on and driving home to bed.

The next morning, I'm still wearing his sweater at breakfast. Grammy glances at it, but doesn't say anything. "Do you want to try surfing today?" asks Papaw. I shrug. Better than just sitting here.

"I guess," I reply.

I go back, change into my suit and rash guard and grab my board, remembering the board Sawyer and I made. I wonder what he did with it. He probably threw it away or put it in his dad's shop for sale.

"Ready," I announce in the living room minutes later. Papaw come with me, and Grammy tags along too. Papaw drives out to Sunset, and thankfully, Sawyer's picked a different spot for today.
I paddle out and get a smooth, clean ride on my first wave. I do a few control exercises on the next wave and spend the rest of the morning trying small airs. That afternoon, I go to see my physical therapist, Kelly.

"Alright, here's the lowdown," Dr. Kelly explains. "Your knee has healed enough that you can surf a little bit. I'd recommend it, actually, to get used to the movements again. But, at this point, I'd say it's extremely risky to try regionals. It's extremely physically demanding, because you will be pushed to do hardest tricks you can. Sorry, Andrea, but it's just not safe."

"Great," I say sarcastically. "Just great."

On the drive home, my mom calls. "Hey, sweetheart, I had a minute and wanted to see what you were up to."

"Oh, nothing," I reply. "Driving home from the physical therapist. What's up with you?"

"Well, I found out that I am due for a vacation, so..." she begins. "I'm coming for your birthday!"

"Really?" I say, excited at the prospect of having some time just to hang out. That is, if she knows what the definition of "vacation" is.

"Really!" she echoes. "I've got to go, but I'll see you in two weeks! I love you!"

"Love you too," I reply. "Bye." I hang up as we go in the house.

Over the next week and a half, my routine goes like this: Get up, go surf, come home, be depressed and aggravated, go to bed. Rinse and repeat. On more than one day, McKayla comes over to help cheer me up, even though she thinks I'm only depressed about my knee and regionals and doesn't know what happened between Sawyer and I. All she knows is that we had a falling out and aren't talking anymore.

Finally, she makes an executive decision to get me out of the house. The two of us hop in the car and end up at the movie theater about twenty minutes later. "What do you want to see?" she inquires as we enter the building.

"Do you even need to ask?" I retort. She smiles.

"Good. Just checking you hadn't been replaced by an alien," she assures. "Two for *Three Hours Too Soon*."

The movie does cheer me up a bit. Unfortunately, the movie doesn't last long and neither does the cheery effect. My phone rings on the way home. "Hello?"

"Hey sweetheart! How's the knee?" My dad greets.

"Hey dad, it's good. What's up?"

"Well, I just sealed a deal with a huge client," he begins. "And I can take a few days off, so I'm coming for your birthday!" he exclaims. My heart drops into my stomach.

"Yay!" I exclaim, internally saying words that would get me grounded for life. "Can't wait!"

"I'll be there in four days and stay for three," he informs.

"Uh, Dad? Have you, I don't know, talked to mom about this?" I inquire, hoping to quench the inevitable fire before it starts.

"No, why?"

"She's coming too," I break the news. I can hear him blow air through his nearly closed lips, puffing them up like he does when he's stressed.

"Alright, I'll call and talk to her," he promises. "It's your birthday. Don't worry about a thing."

"Okay," I agree hesitantly. "Love you."

"Love you too. Bye."

Well, this is going to be the most interesting birthday ever.

My parents haven't been in the same room since they got divorced. They avoid talking to each other as much as possible, so three days in the same house will be… oh, who am I kidding, it could be a nuclear disaster.

"What's the matter?" inquires Mac.

"Both of my parents are coming for my birthday," I state.

"Oh… Oh!" she responds, making a worried face at me. "Happy Birthday, I guess." We laugh, as the alternative is to worry and my father clearly instructed me not to do that. *"Happy Birthday, honey. I'm starting a war for your birthday! Don't worry, it'll be fine!"*

She drops me off at my house and wishes me luck as I head in.

"Hey, I'm back," I call from the entryway.

"Hi, honey," Grammy calls. "In the kitchen."

"Did my parents call you?" I inquire, entering the vanilla-scented room.

"Well, your mother called a few weeks ago about staying here for your birthday. Your dad called this morning about the same thing," she answers. I purse my lips and nod. "Have you talked to them?"

"Yep. Mom called me a week and a half ago, and Dad called me on the way home from the movie," I inform.

"Do you want them both to stay here? I didn't say anything to them about each other."

"I told Dad. He said he'd talk to Mom." I head to the fridge and grab a can of Dr. Pepper, popping the tab and settling in on the couch.

"So is there anyone you'd like to have over on your birthday?" she inquires.

"Maybe Mac," I suggest. "Or maybe not. Maybe we'll just do a family thing." So my best friend doesn't have to witness our catastrophic meltdown.

"What about Sawyer?" she inquires. She had to bring him up.

"No," I reply immediately. Yes, of course. Throw him into the mix. Make me really go nuts for my birthday. "I'll be back," I stall, heading back to my room. I lean against the closed door for a moment and notice my board in the corner. The green hunk of foam reminds me of the board Sawyer made me. I still don't know what he did with it. I wish I didn't care.

It's not that I care about the board. My parents would probably buy me another one exactly like it. The problem is it wouldn't be exactly like it, because he didn't shape the rails. His hands didn't guide mine in forming the foam. He didn't make it. It's like the sweater. I wouldn't care about it for the most part, except that when I wear it, I feel like I'm back in his arms. I wish I didn't care about these things, but I do. I can't seem to stop caring, no matter what I try. I've tried to hate him, but all his name causes is an ache in my chest and a question in the back of my mind:

What if it did work?

SIXTEEN

"Hi sweetheart," my mother greets, waving on the right side my computer screen. My dad does the same on the left.

"Hi," I say, smiling and waving back. "Okay, you said you wanted to talk to me at the same time?"

"Yeah. It's about your birthday," Dad begins. I nod, urging him on. "We know it's been a long time since we've been in the same place, and we know that it's going to be challenging, but we've called a truce for your birthday. This is about you, not us, and if you want both of us there, we'll both come."

"I'd love to have both of you here," I answer. "You'll really call a truce for me?"

"We promise," Mom swears.

"We decided we'll come for three days: tomorrow, your birthday and the day after,"

"Alright then," I decide. "I'll see you both tomorrow."

I click a few buttons and their images disappear. I take a deep breath and try to convince myself it will be okay. They're calling a truce for my birthday, and if there's one thing they can't stand, it's when my birthday isn't perfect. I could've cared less if the pony at my tenth birthday party was white or grey, but my mother's persistence that it had to be white is evidence that this might actually work because of that kind of dedication to making my birthday good.

The next morning I wake up on the right side of the bed, confident that this week is going to be fantastic. I pull on a pair of dark jean cutoff shorts and my black Carrie Underwood *Blown Away Tour* shirt and head out to the kitchen. "Morning," I sing.

"You're awfully cheery this morning," Papaw observes.

"Excited for Mom and Dad?" Grammy guesses. I nod. "Some packages came in the mail today. I guess your parents mailed your gifts here ahead of time." Uh-oh.

This is the one thing that could be the most dangerous to the truce. Like I said earlier, they compete with each other about gifts.

Who's is bigger, who's I like better, who's is more expensive, the stuff little kids care about.

"So what do you want to do for the big day tomorrow?" Papaw asks.

"Well, we're doing lettuce wraps for dinner," I begin listing. "Maybe we could watch a movie or something?" Papaw nods and looks at me as if telling me to keep going. "I don't know, we could go bowling in the afternoon?"

"That's a good idea," Grammy comments. "Maybe that's what McKayla could come do with us." I nod.

A few hours later, I shove my feet in my rubber slippers and hop in the car to venture to the airport. At the baggage claim, my mother opens her arms to me, which I run into gratefully. For all the complaints I make about her, she's still my mom and nothing quite feels the same as a mother's hug. Pulling back, she looks at me worriedly. "What's wrong?"

"Nothing," I reply innocently. "I'm fine." She smiles and pulls me in for another hug.

"Happy birthday, my sweet girl," she says.

"Thanks, Mom," I reply. Over her shoulder, I see my dad with his business attire on. As I pull back and let mom get her bags, I wave to him. When he gets closer, he opens his arms and I run to him like I would when I was little. He lifts me up like it's nothing and then pulls me into a hug.

"I don't know how you can do that to an adult," I tease, smiling smugly.

"You're not an adult yet," he corrects. "You still have twenty four hours left of being a kid." I laugh and follow the rest of the group.

"So, tell me all about what's been happening this summer," my mom demands, smiling from the back seat of the old beater.

"Well, Mac and I have had fun hanging out," I begin. "And I won two divisions at my first competition, and one in my second. Other than that, it's been a pretty chill time."

"Now, wait, I want to hear the epic tale of what exactly happened to that knee of yours," Dad interjects.

"You remember Sally Emerson, right?" I inquire. They both nod. "So I was at a birthday party for a friend of mine and he and I were just hanging out talking, when Sally dared me to walk the ridgepole of his garage to prove I was brave, so I did and I made it to the end. But then she wouldn't give me the ladder and told me to walk back to the other end with the ladder to get down. I was almost at the end and I twisted my foot in a weird way and it hurt my knee, so I fell and hit my knee on the edge of the garage roof."

"Why does it not surprise me that it was Sally?" my Dad laughs. "You two were always at odds with each other."

"So who's birthday party was it?" Mom inquires.

"Oh, it was the, um, the boy that came to see me in the hospital," I reply, remembering her call in the middle of *Divergent*. "Sawyer."

"Oh, the complicated one?" she hints, smiling.

"Yeah."

"Has it gotten any less complicated?"

"Nope," I respond bluntly. "In fact, it's gotten more complicated than ever." She purses her lips.

"Complicated? A boy? I don't like the sound of that," Dad jokes. "What did he do? Do I need to beat him up?"

"No, Dad," I laugh. "Trust me, it's fine. We don't even talk to each other any more."

We arrive home and let Mom and Dad get settled, while I help Grammy with her Char-siu. Dad heads out to the garage with Papaw to take a look at the bikes he's working on. Mom pulls me aside and asks to talk to me back in my room.

"What's up, Mom?" I inquire.

"I want to hear more about your summer," she chides. "Come on." She pats the spot next to her on the bed and I cross the room to sit down.

"What do you want to know?"

"For starters, what happened with you and this Sawyer boy?" she asks. I sigh.

"Really, it was nothing," I reply, trying to fend her off.

"I just want to help, if I can," she prods.

"The reason I said it was complicated was because we got off on the wrong foot," I begin. "Then after a while, we became friends. We had a falling out a few weeks ago and haven't talked since."

"I'm sorry that happened," she comforts after a moment of silence.

"It's okay," I reply. "I'm over it."

We end up making it all night with only a few stressed faces from either of my parents, which gives me hope that maybe it won't be a catastrophic meltdown.

It's weird how one thing can worm it's way into your mind and stick there. When I'm just laying here in the dark, the one thing that has stuck in my mind is the only thing in my mind and has been for weeks. Finally, I kick off my covers, take off my shirt and pull Sawyer's sweater over my head. The warm knit fabric envelopes me and, even though I've had it almost a month, still smells vaguely like him. I feel as though I might cry.

Instead, though, I simply twist the sleeves around my fingers and close my eyes, trying to convince myself that I did what I was going to have to do eventually. The nagging thought in my mind, though, is what I had to do.

I broke his heart.

SEVENTEEN

I am eighteen. I am an actual, legitimate adult.

I sit up, yawn and stretch. Standing, I stumble out to the kitchen and take a seat at the bar. "Happy birthday, sweetheart," Grammy says with a smile.

"Morning birthday girl," Dad greets. He's dressed a little more casually for today, wearing jeans and a t-shirt instead of his typical business outfit.

"Hi," I reply. "Mom still asleep?"

"Yes, and Papaw's in the garage working on something," Grammy answers with a twinkle in her eye.

Grammy dishes me up a plate full of chocolate chip waffles and a cup of orange juice as I hear the click of high heels on the wooden hallway floor. Mom's not asleep now. Not unless she looks like a business-y Coco Chanel when she sleeps. She's dressed in a sleeveless white blouse with a cowl neck, paired with a red pencil skirt and red Louboutin pumps. Her makeup is flawlessly done, the colors precisely chosen to match the outfit.

I hate it. I hate every speck of professionalism in her manner as she walks towards the bar to sit next to me. I hate the fact that there's not a hair out of place, not a wrinkle in her clothes. But she's trying. She's here, isn't she? "Happy birthday, baby girl!" she says excitedly. I smile and return her hug when she opens her arms for one. She looks strangely at my sweater. "I don't recognize that sweater. Where'd you get it?"

"A friend gave it to me," I reply, internally questioning if it's the truth.

She turns down Grammy's waffles, opting for a cup of coffee and some kind of oatmeal-looking mush, explaining to Grammy all about her diet. I call it the EBN diet (the Eat Basically Nothing diet). No gluten, dairy, eggs, peanuts, sugar or artificial sweeteners. Not me. I'll stick with actual food, thanks.

The doorbell rings approximately eleven times before we leave to go have lunch at Tara's, every single one being a package or delivery of some sort that one of my parents take back to his or her bedroom. McKayla and her family are the twelfth ring, ready to go to lunch and go bowling. Tara's is fun, and my parents even show a little glimpse of their pre-divorce selves when greeted by some old friends. They converse easily and my mother actually relaxes a little bit. She still turns down the bowling though, in favor of watching, so Mac, her little brother, my dad, Mr. Atwood, Mrs. Atwood, Papaw, Grammy and I all duke it out in two games of bowling. I'm a terrible bowler, but it's still fun.

When we get back, Grammy kicks it into high gear in the kitchen, making my favorite Chinese lettuce wraps for dinner. They sound like some veggie dish, right? Wrong. It's this spicy filling of ground chicken, onions, water chestnuts and some other vegetables, wrapped in a leaf of lettuce topped with a sweet and spicy sauce. It's amazing.

After dinner, we have cake and ice cream, then my parents go back to their rooms and bring out tons of boxes and bags, all brightly (and commercially) wrapped. Grammy and Papaw add another package to the mix and bid me to start opening. I pick the package closest to me which is tagged "Love, Mom" and start ripping the paper, revealing a big box full of perfumes like the whole "Daisy" line by Marc Jacobs, Taylor Swift's new fragrance and One Direction's new scent. I smile and thank her, being careful to select a box from Dad next. Inside is a tutorial book on how to dye your hair and a box full of dyes, from plain bleach, to bright pink, all the way to midnight blue. I don't know what gave him the impression I wanted that, but I smile and thank him anyway.

The rest of the boxes contain lots of instant film for my Polaroid camera and few photography books, lots of makeup, a set of Beats by Dre studio headphones, two boxes of clothes and shoes and a collection of gift cards.

Finally, my Dad hands me an envelope as his last gift. "Now, there's only one, because I just couldn't leave my company for that long, but I figured you'd still want to go," he explains. I slit the top curiously and pull out a sheet of paper that contains the information for what looks like a trip to Australia. My heart soars, even before I notice the dates.

"Is this for real?" I inquire.

"Pull out the next page," he instructs. I do so and find the ticket information for one ticket to the Quicksilver Pro Gold Coast. No. Way.

"What is it, honey?" my mother inquires in a voice she's fighting to keep sweet.

"I'm going to Australia for the Quicksilver Pro!" I exclaim. My mother's mouth drops open slightly and she glances at my father.

"Australia?" she repeats.

"It's only for two weeks," my father assures her. I hand her the papers and she immediately reads them.

"It's in the middle of the school year," she protests. "You can't leave in the middle of your senior year for two weeks just for some surf competition!" My heart sinks, and not just because she said I can't go. I feel my eyes start to sting.

"Some surf competition?" my father echoes. "Hold on just a second, you pull her from school and take her to Paris, Milan, London and New York Fashion Week almost every year and now, suddenly, I'm evil for taking her somewhere she actually wants to go?"

"Please," I whisper, unable to speak thanks to the lump in my throat.

"First of all, you're not taking her," she argues. "You provided the ticket. I actually go with her to the shows during Fashion Week, which, by the way, is a cultural experience that adds to her education. You're just shipping her off to Australia by herself and I won't allow it!"

"I'm her parent too, I don't need you to tell me what's okay for my daughter!"

"Please, just stop," I whimper, but their shouts drown me out.

"Your daughter?!" she shouts. "She's not 'your daughter!' I've taken over her education enti-"

"She is my daughter! I take her for the whole summer and holidays and-"

"ENOUGH!" I shout, standing. I can feel hot tears rolling down my face. They both look at me like children who've been caught doing something they shouldn't. Seeing my tears my mother comes over to comfort me.

"Sweetheart, I'm so sorry, it's just-"

"No," I cut her off, pushing away her outstretched arms. She stands there, arms open wide for a moment, too shocked to move. Slowly she puts her arms down. "You don't get to just decide to show up in my life and be the picture-perfect mother you think you are. You can't possibly think a few five minute conversations and trips to fashion shows I didn't even want to go to count as motherly affection. You're not the woman in my baby pictures. You're someone who looks vaguely like her, but doesn't have a daughter. At least, not unless you feel like acknowledging my existence."

I turn to my father, all the aggravation of the past eighteen years welling up inside me and finally spilling over. "And you can't argue that I'm your daughter, either," I start in. "You carve out a few minutes every few weeks to call me, and you take me on one or two afternoon sightseeing trips when I'm there in the summer. You don't do anything to deserve the title of 'Father' to me. You don't even remember what I talk to you about when we do have a conversation. Out of everyone in this room, the people who are the most like parents to me are Grammy and Papaw. You two may be my blood parents, but even before the divorce, I practically lived here. Then you took me away from that and I had no one."

I look at my mom, who is still dumbstruck at my outpour of feelings. "You want to know what happened this summer? What's wrong? I fell in love. He loved me through everything. Even when I hated him, he loved me. Then I broke his heart. You know why? Because my parents broke each other's hearts and made my life what it is. I swore I would never do that to anyone. You two promised to love each other forever when you got married and you thought signing some papers could fix what broke, but you were wrong. You two turned me off from even the idea of love. You made me scared of it.

I didn't want what happened to you two to happen to me, but what I didn't realize is that it didn't just happen to you. You made it happen. You chose it. And I've made what possibly could've been the worst decision of my life because of it. So, thanks for all the gifts, but you don't have to argue over me anymore. I'm done."

And with that, I grab the keys to Gertrude off the hook and slam the door behind me, not caring if anyone comes after me or not.

EIGHTEEN

I gun the engine, floor the pedal and don't look back. You might think what I said was mean, but there's a reason they call it "the ugly truth."

The sad thing was I actually thought they were going to make it my whole birthday without fighting. They tried so hard and it all ended in nuclear warfare. But hey, you know, I got some perfume and some clothes, so who cares? Zipidi-do-da. Oh, and don't forget, tickets to an event that just ruined my birthday that I'm not even going to get to go to.

Somehow, I end up at Banzai Pipeline. I park the bike and just go sit on the sand, watching the surf. Just when I think the tears might be gone, a wave of them even bigger than the ones rolling in at my feet comes on and I just pull my knees into my chest and cry. Sometimes, that's all there is left to do.

I don't know how long I sit here, but it's a considerable amount of time. Even after the tears stop, I sit here listening to the waves and thinking about how messed up my life is.

"Mind if I camp here?"

My head slowly lifts to meet a familiar pair of deep, shining blue eyes. I shake my head and Sawyer sits down on the sand beside me. After a little pause, he says "I'm glad I gave you that sweater. It definitely looks better on you than it ever did on me." I use the sleeves to dry my eyes.

"How did you find me?" I inquire.

"I wasn't looking for you," he replies. "I just came to surf."

"Oh." I nod.

"Happy birthday, by the way." He nudges my shoulder with his playfully.

"You remembered?"

"You really think I'd forget?" That sweet smile I've come to love flashes across his face for a moment, then disappears again. "Also, you left this at my my house a few weeks ago," he informs, handing me my copy of *Three Hours Too Soon*.

"Thanks," I reply, taking it. Our fingers brush in the encounter and I am tempted not to let go.

"You know, I just realized something," he says after a short silence.

"What?" I ask.

"I don't think I've ever seen you without a surfboard or a book in your hand," he says. I laugh. "Seriously though, why do you read so much?"

I pause, unsure of how to put it. "Love is better in books," I finally answer.

"Explain."

"Happily ever afters exist," I start after a moment. "Tragedies are so depressing they can only go up from the ending, and people have to converse or there would be no story. Every book I've ever read is better than my own life. Even books like *Three Hours Too Soon*. Jane has leukemia, yes, but she also has parents that love her and practically hang on her every word. She has a boyfriend that through all, will continue to love her even when she can't love him. A girl with cancer's life is better than my own." He is quiet for a moment.

"Does this have something to do with your parents?" he asks.

"Something?" I laugh coldly. "More like everything." I take a deep breath. "My parents got divorced when I was nine, but haven't really cared about me since birth. I'm an inconvenience, an extra piece of luggage they can't always check. Then they decide they do care about me and go crazy, competing to be the better parent and in doing so, are actually terrible parents. I don't know if they even really love me, and they've made me afraid to love anyone else."

He stares out at the sea. "No one should be afraid of love," he finally responds. "No one should have to go through life never being loved or loving anyone else." Another silence ensues.

"I didn't mean to interrupt your surf time," I say apologetically.

"You're fine. Actually," he counters. "I was only going surfing to get this amazing girl off my mind." I smile and look down at my hands. "So why are you out here? It's your birthday, you should be celebrating."

"My parents both came for my birthday," I reply. "They called a truce, but couldn't keep it and when they started to fight right in the middle of the living room, all the feelings of the past eighteen years boiled over and I let them have it, then came out here. I highly suspect they're going to come looking for me and tell me that was wrong or immature or something any minute now."

"So, I still don't get why you didn't tell them I kicked you in the eye," he says. "That day, they called you as you were lying on the couch with the ice pack on your face and you didn't tell them I kicked you."

"I told you. I didn't want them to worry," I reply. "I didn't want them going all crazy parents on me, buying me junk I don't need like I'm some little kid that will feel better with one trip to the toy store."

"Ah."

"Yeah."

"Look, I want to say I'm sorry," he begins. "If I'd known a few weeks ago, I wouldn't have just tried to kiss you out of the blue. I get it now. I understand why you don't like me like that." I nod, not knowing what to say between what I want to say and the walls of fear encompassing me, keeping me from coming out with it. He stands up to leave. "If I can't, I hope someone will break through this idea of love that you have someday. Like I said, no one deserves that."

My head and my heart fight for control of my mouth. As he walks away, something stirs inside of me and suddenly I know exactly what to say.

"Sawyer!" I shout. He turns back to me and I jog a few paces to catch up to him. "You know what? I'm done," I state nervously. "I was stupid and scared enough to let you go once." I take a deep breath. "The truth is that I love you," I confess. "When I realized what I'd done, I cried myself to sleep that night, and for almost a week afterwards. I couldn't stop thinking about you and the only conclusion I came to was that if the way you loved me isn't true love, then it really doesn't exist." He stands, speechless for a moment. "I love you. I'm so sorry that I was such a jerk towards you and that I was too caught up in myself to see that you really did love me. And I'm sorry if I'm too late."

"You could never be too late," he assures, wrapping me in his arms for a tight hug. "Because I love you too." He pulls back to look at me and tucks a stray lock of hair behind my ear, caressing my face gently. Slowly, he leans his face in towards mine and this time, I don't turn away. His lips fit to mine perfectly as my walls of fear shatters in one fell blow. As we pull apart, I say a silent prayer, more sure someone will hear it this time: *Thank you. Thank you for not abandoning me. I see what you were doing now. You knew. You had the cards all along.*

Sawyer smiles coyly. "So, Miss Maverick. Would you like to go on a date with me?"

"I would love to," I reply, smiling back. He picks me up and swings me around as I giggle, setting me down gently. "One of us is going to have to change, though, because I can't go surfing like this, and you can't go out anywhere like that." I gesture to his rash guard and board shorts.

"That's fine," he agrees with a twinkle in his eye. "I have to go pick up something for my girlfriend, anyway. It's her birthday today, you know."

"Really? Sounds like a lovely girl," I joke.

"Oh, she is," he replies, pressing his lips to my forehead for a moment. "She's amazing."

"So what do you want to do?" I inquire as he entwines his fingers with mine.

"I was thinking a movie," he suggests.

"What movie?" I ask.

"The one I cried like a baby during," he replies, making me laugh.

"I knew you cried!"

"You have to be inhuman not to cry during *Three Hours Too Soon*," he defends. I laugh again and lean my head against his shoulder.

He packs up and drives back to his house to change and pick me up for a movie in a little while. I, meanwhile, have some unfinished business back at the house. I ride Gertrude back home and set the keys on the hook just inside the door upon arrival. "Honey? Is that you?" my mother's voice calls.

I enter the living room, where it seems no one has moved, except my mother's makeup is smudged and my father's eyes are red.

"Okay, look," I begin after a moment, as no one else apparently wants to start. "I was wrong to blow up at you guys like that, and I'm sorry. I really am. I can't say I didn't mean it, though. That would make me a liar." I take a deep breath, to keep myself composed. "Even before the divorce, I felt like I was an inconvenience to you two. The way I was always either at school or here, the way you didn't want to see me when I was there, and the way you fought about me."

My mother claps a hand to her mouth. "You heard us?"

"I'm pretty sure the whole island heard you two debate who wanted to have kids in the first place," I reply harshly. "You weren't exactly quiet, and it's kind of hard for a seven year old girl to sleep when her parents are screaming at each other down the hall." I take a deep breath and pause, unsure of what to say next. "I know you two try to be good parents, but you made your choices when you split: your work was the top priority. Everything else came second. I marvel at that baby album back in New York sometimes."

"Why?" my mother asks, puzzled.

"Because in the pictures in that scrapbook, you were the mom that I needed," I explain, tearing up again. "You wore t-shirts and sweatpants. You didn't wear makeup every waking second of the day. You put your hair up in a messy ponytail just to keep it out of your face, instead of these fancy up-dos. You weren't the top Mary Kay seller. You weren't traveling and speaking at conventions and going to fashion shows every week. You were just happy being my mom."

Tears are rolling down my mother's face, smudging her makeup even more. "Sweetheart," she begins. She stands and pulls me into a tight hug. "I'm so sorry," she whispers. "I am happy being your mom, but I made a lot of bad decisions that made it seem like I'm not. I'm so sorry. Can you ever forgive me?"

"Of course I can," I reply, hugging her back. "That's what families do. They don't split up. They don't hate each other. They forgive each other and move on and are stronger." I pull back and turn to my dad, who stands and looks at me with tears in his eyes.

"You're right," he says. "I don't deserve to be called your father. I've made some terrible choices and I hope you can see that we really do love you. I'm truly sorry." He smiles at me tearfully. "You really have grown up, my little surfer girl."

"Oh, daddy," I say, the tears in my own eyes finally spilling over. I run into his arms. "I forgive you. And I know you love me. I see that now."

Pulling back, I am unsure where my family will go from here, but for now, I feel like I'm soaring. The weight my previous rant relieved me of has now been lightened even more. Just when I think it isn't physically possible to be any happier, the doorbell rings.

"If you'll excuse me," I say, unable to contain my grin as I wipe my eyes. "I have a date." Grammy bursts into a smile almost as big as mine and my mother smiles. I cross to the foyer and open the door to reveal my very handsome boyfriend, who, like I mentioned before, can do a lot in twenty minutes. He's cleaned up and is wearing the same red polo he wore for his birthday party, paired with khaki shorts. "Hi," I greet, still beaming. "I feel underdressed."

"Hi," he replies, stepping over the threshold. "You shouldn't. You make that sweater look prettier than a prom dress. I didn't have a tuxedo lying around and I couldn't get one in twenty minutes." I laugh. Suddenly, I remember my family is standing behind me.

"Oh, Sawyer, you've met my grandparents," I begin. Grammy and Papaw wave. "And these are my parents. Mom, Dad, this is Sawyer." My father steps forward and holds out his hand. Sawyer shakes it.

"Nice to meet you, son," he greets. "You can call me Sean."

"It's nice to meet you too, sir," Sawyer returns politely.

"I'm Charlotte," my mother introduces. "My daughter's told me a lot about you."

"Really, now? Has she?" he says, quirking an eyebrow at me. "Well, we'd better be going, but I do have one thing I have to do." He takes my hand and says "Close your eyes." I do as he says and follow him, clutching tightly to his hand. He lets go and after a second says "Okay, open them."

I open my eyes to reveal the board he made for me, completely finished and painted light teal, with beautifully hand-painted red roses down the rails. "Oh, Sawyer, it's gorgeous," I breathe, tracing my fingers lightly over the flowers.

"I can't take credit for the flowers," he admits. "I painted it teal, but Julia has a knack for detail. She insisted on roses."

"They're beautiful," I compliment. "Thank you." He takes my hand in his and kisses my cheek.

"A beautiful board for a beautiful girl," he rationalizes. I laugh and lean my head against his shoulder. "Come on, we should get going. Our movie's going to start soon."

"Have fun sweetheart," Grammy says, waving from the doorway with my mother. I wave back and Sawyer leans the board up against the interior garage wall before climbing into the Jeep.

When I rode in this Jeep for the first time, I never wanted to ride in it again. Now, I couldn't be happier to be back in it.

NINETEEN

"Two cherry/blue raspberry Icees and a Sour Patch Kids," Sawyer orders at the movie theater snack bar, without even needing to ask. He carries the drinks and candy into the theater and follows me to a pair of seats in the middle of the dark room. Only a few other people are here, as most movie watchers likely came to see *Three Hours Too Soon* a month or more ago. It is Saturday night, however, so I assumed the theater wouldn't be totally empty.

"Can I tell you something?" Sawyer asks quietly as the previews begin. I nod and he kisses me by surprise.

"I wanted to do that the first time we saw this movie," he whispers as we pull apart. I grin and lace my fingers in his as he turns back to the screen, leaning my head on his shoulder.

Two and a half hours and lots of tears later, the lights in the theater come up and he takes me home. I wave goodnight to him from the doorway, and as soon as I am inside, I close the door, lean against it and sigh happily. Then I hear something that makes me curious. It's a light, loud, happy sound that I haven't heard authentically in a long time.

I enter the living room to see my mother doubled over in laughter on the couch without a speck of makeup on her face. Her hair is in a ponytail and (horror of all horrors) she's wearing sweatpants. My mother owns sweatpants?

My face must look pretty funny, because my grandmother laughs heartily and says "Close your mouth, dear, it's not becoming." I close my mouth and blink a few times to make sure I'm not hallucinating.

"You own sweatpants?" I ask in disbelief.

"They're your grandmother's," she replies. "But I am buying some as soon as I can. I don't remember when I've been this comfortable."

"Well, you've never looked more beautiful," I assure her truthfully. She smiles.

"So tell me," she starts excitedly as I collapse onto the couch beside her. She sits up eagerly, crossing her legs indian-style and leaning forward. "I want to hear all about Sawyer and your date."

"I want to know how you went from not speaking to dating," Grammy adds.

I launch into the many ups and downs of our relationship, from the day he kicked me in the face to the moment he dropped me off a little while ago. Both my parents and grandparents laugh and generally enjoy themselves throughout the whole story, and by the end, my dad says "It sounds like you picked a good one." A thought that has been present at the back of my mind comes to the tip of my tongue at that moment.

"I wish I could just stay here," I let slip. My mom glances at my dad in a funny way. "What?" I inquire.

"We were talking while you were gone," my dad begins.

"And we decided that if you'd like to, you can finish school here," Mom continues. My mouth drops open in disbelief again.

"And," my dad adds, "you can stay here afterwards if you want. You don't have to keep going back and forth. You can pick one place and stay, just so long as we can visit you whenever we have time."

"Are you serious?" I ask in disbelief.

"There's no reason not to," Dad replies.

"You're obviously happiest here," Mom agrees. "You've got Grammy, Papaw, McKayla, Sawyer and all your friends here. You don't have to make the decision now, but I can stay and help you find a place over the next week if you'd like."

"I can't imagine anything better in the whole world," I state. "And I would miss both of you lots, but you're welcome to visit anytime you like."

"Then it's settled," Dad announces. "You can stay here for your last year of school and see where this crazy road takes you from there."

I shower and change into pajamas after bidding everyone goodnight, but before I fall asleep, I text Sawyer. "I need to talk to you tomorrow. I have big news :-)"

"Alright then. I'd better get some sleep. I have something to tell you too ;) See you at breakfast tomorrow? My house?" he replies a minute later. I smile and text "Okay. Goodnight :-)" to which he replies "Goodnight beautiful :-)"

The next morning, I ride Gertrude over to the Hensleys' house. Melissa greets me at the door, and Julia waves from the table.

"Morning," I yawn, smiling and waving back afterwards. As I cross to the table, Sawyer runs down the hallway, yelling at the top of his lungs, with Daniel on his tail. Daniel is carrying a pillow above his head like a club. "What the…?" I say, trailing off into laughter.

"Little boys never grow up," Melissa states, shaking her head and smiling.

"Oh, hi! Andrea! You're here!" shout Sawyer. "My brother's trying to kill me!"

"Okay," I reply nonchalantly. "I'll say some nice things at your funeral."

"'Kay, thanks for the help, love you too," he replies sarcastically, ducking behind my chair at the table. I laugh again and my heart flutters a tiny bit upon hearing him say "love you."

"Okay, we're done," Melissa calls, putting a stop to the ruckus. Daniel chucks the pillow at the couch in the living room and drops into a chair at the table. Sawyer collapses next to me, laughing.

"For the record, I do love you. A lot," I tell him, pecking his cheek.

"I know. I love you too," he replies, lacing his fingers with mine. "Now. Awesome news you texted me about last night?"

"Right," I remember excitedly. "So, while we were at the movies last night, my parents were talking, and they decided that instead of going back to New York for the whole school year and going to the college of my mother's choice and all that, I'm only going back for a week or two."

"Okay, that's cool," he replies. "So… why are you only going back for a week or two?"

"Well, that's the next part," I continue. "I'm only going back to New York for a week or two just to say goodbye to some friends, pack up my things and send them here."

"Say goodbye? Pack up?" he repeats, puzzled.

"Yeah, so I can come live here," I answer. "Mom and Dad said I can finish high school here and stick around as long as I like." I bite my lip and wait for his reaction.

"Wait, wait, like, you're not leaving? You're staying here? Forever?" he says, mouth slightly open and eyes wide.

"Yes, Sawyer. I'm staying here. Forever," I answer, laughing. Instead of answering, he smiles wide and kisses me, right there in front of everyone. When he pulls back, I giggle. "I take it you like the news."

"It is the best news I've heard since I don't know when," he laughs, leaning his forehead against mine.

"Ugh, do you have to do that in the kitchen?" Daniel groans. "My brother, the lovestruck goof. Who would've thought?"

"Hey, I think it's cute," Julia interjects. I smile at her and suddenly remember the flowers.

"By the way, thank you for painting my board," I tell her. "It looks amazing."

"You're welcome," she replies shyly. "Painting is just something I love to do."

"Well, you're great at it," I compliment honestly. "Maybe I should get your autograph." I wink at her and she beams.

"So who've you told so far?" Melissa asks.

"Just you guys, my parents and my grandparents know," I answer. "I have to go tell McKayla soon."

"Are you going to stay with your grandparents?" Sawyer inquires.

"Actually, my mom is staying a few extra days to help me find my own place and get things sorted out," I respond.

"You're own place," Daniel repeats. "Sweet. Sounds legit."

Totally off subject, but this is yet another concept I simply do not understand. Why take a word like "legitimate" and turn it into some stupid slang term? Literally, what you are telling me is that it sounds lawful for me to have my own place. Whatever. Misuse the english language all you want. It's not like anyone actually pays attention to it anymore.

"Are you going to get an apartment or a house?" Sawyer inquires. "And why not stay at your grandparents house?"

"I have absolutely no idea for the first one and the second, I'm getting my own place because my parents want me to 'be independent' or something like that. I figure I'll need to have my own workout space anyway," I reply. "After all, a professional surfer has to have appropriate training equipment. Plus, a friend of mine from New York will definitely come stay as often as she can, and I'm considering finally getting a pet. Grammy likes animals, as long as they're not in her house. I have to go start working out the details with my mom, but I have to tell Mac first. Do you all want to come over for dinner tonight?"

"Definitely," Sawyer replies. Melissa nods. "But— rewind there. Professional surfer?"

I nod. "I sent the forms in today to apply for an ASP membership. If I get accepted, I'll make my ASP debut at the Pro Curl in January."

"What a coincidence!" Sawyer smiles devilishly. "Mum, could you get my letter for a second?" Melissa hands him an opened envelope. "You see, I just so happened to get a letter back yesterday from the ASP. I applied on my birthday for membership." He holds out the unfolded papers.

Dear Mr. Hensley,

Thank you for your application and congratulations on your many amateur wins. We look forward to seeing similar results from you in the Association of Surfing Professionals…

I stop there because the rest of the letter details regulations, member information, etc. I look up at Sawyer, open-mouthed. He bites his lower lip, smiles and raises his eyebrows in question.

"What?!" I finally choke out. "Oh my gosh, Sawyer, this is amazing! Congratulations!"

"Thanks," he says modestly. He takes the letter back and hands it to his mom. "I'm pretty stoked about it."

"Yeah! You're an ASP member! You should be stoked!"

"Don't act like it's some gigantic deal," he says, smiling. "You're going to get the same letter in a month or two."

"It is a gigantic deal, though," I counter. "And it's not for sure that I'll get in."

"Of course you'll get in. Who could say no to skilled *and* gorgeous surfer girl?"

After Melissa's scrumptious toast, bacon and egg breakfast, I bid everyone goodbye until tonight, ride back home and cross the street to McKayla's house. Mrs. Atwood answers the door and informs me that McKayla is in her room, sleeping in. I make my way through the hall and into her bedroom quietly, then pounce on her. "Wake up sleepyhead!" I shout. She starts to yell and then realizes it's me.

"What the heck was that for?!" Mac exclaims.

"For sleeping in when I have the biggest news ever to tell you!" I cry.

"What news?" she gasps, sitting up.

"Big announcement number 1: I'm moving!" I yell.

"Okay…" she says unsurely.

"Here!" I finish. Her mouth drops open.

"Like… for real? You're moving here permanently?" she inquires, dumbstruck. "Going to school and everything?"

"Yep." She grins and tackles me in a hug. "Wait! There's more!"

"Really?"

"Big announcement number 2:" I continue. "You kinda… sorta… just maybe… might have been a little bit right."

"Okay, say that again in normal english," she replies.

"You were right," I repeat. "Sawyer did like me. He loves me."

"Wait, 'loves?' Present tense?" she clarifies hopefully. I purse my lips, trying to hide my grin and nod. She squeals, then laughs and hugs me again. "I told you!"

"I know, I know," I reply. "I was wrong. Thankfully, I realized it before I made a giant mistake."

"I need details."

I laugh and start from the beginning of the fight yesterday. She's a good listener, and she sighs, laughs and gasps in all the right spots of the story. At the end, she just grins wide and repeats her earlier statement: "I told you so."

A moment later, my phone rings. "Jerkface" is calling me. I laugh at the caller ID, which I haven't changed since the day he put it in. "Hello?"

"Just out of curiosity, if you were going to buy a dog, what kind would you get?" Sawyer inquires. "Like, big? Little? Medium? Long hair? Short hair?"

"I don't care about the hair length as much, but I would want one that would be easy to groom," I reply. "And not a Chihuahua, but no bigger than a Border Collie. Why are you all of a sudden curious about this?"

"No reason," he responds casually. "I just remembered you said you wanted one and wondered what kind."

"Okay then. See you later."

"Love you. See you at dinner."

"I love you too. Bye." I hang up and McKayla's grin says it all. I roll my eyes. "Yep. You definitely told me so," I admit.

Later that day, I check my email for a few of the real estate links my mom sent me. Scrolling through, I notice an email from my english teacher back in New York, Mr. Clarke.

"Dear Miss Maverick,

Earlier today, I received my finalized class lists. You seem not to be on any of them. I recall you saying you would be back unless something drastic happened before you left. I expect a five page narrative essay on what happened, so as to have an answer when Miss Carver begins to question me.

Sincerely,

Mr. Clarke."

I laugh, but before I can respond, my phone begins to sing.

"Hello?"

"Okay, this summer officially blows," Amy greets depressingly.

"Uh-oh. What happened?"

"Logan's a freaking idiot, that's what."

"Ah."

"He started going out with Sarah Durst. *Before* he dumped me. I walked in on them kissing and he gave me the most cliche line ever — 'it's not what you think'— and I smacked him. So, yeah, we're over."

"Woah, woah, back it up— you smacked him?" I repeat incredulously.

"Yeah," she admits. "He deserved it."

"You won't hear me arguing," I reply. "So..." I try to think of how to approach what I was going to call and tell her anyway.

"So how has your summer been?" she inquires.

"Good," I begin. "Actually, that's a lie. It's been fantastic and awful."

"Um, okay... Explanation please?"

"Well, my first day back, I got kicked in the eye when I was surfing by this guy named Sawyer," I launch into my tale. "I thought he was a total jerk, but then we sort of became friends, then I realized I liked him and people kept telling me he liked me and I was jerk to him and we quit talking, then after a giant blow-up at my parents, I was on the beach, crying and he came and told me he still loved me."

"Oh. My. Gosh. What did you do?" Amy asks eagerly.

"I told him I loved him too and we went out on our first date last night," I reply. Amy squeals and I laugh.

"You fell in love?! AND YOU DIDN'T TELL ME?!" she exclaims.

"I did tell you! Just now!" I return. "I also dislocated my knee and had surgery. But, the good news is I have completely normal knees now."

"Ouch. Surfing?"

"I fell off a roof."

"Okay then. You really did have a crazy summer. So, when are you coming back?"

"Actually, I was going to call you just as you called me," I reply. "Amy, I'm staying in Oahu."

"What?"

"I'm getting my own place here in Oahu and I'm staying. I'll finish school here and I'll be able to actually train for a pro surfing career." Amy sighs and it's quiet for a moment.

"Okay, you can leave on two conditions:" she demands. "You're place has to have a guest room and I have to be able to come and visit."

"Done," I reply, laughing a bit. "First visit is winter break. Don't miss it."

"I won't. So, tell me about this boyfriend of yours!"

"You're going to freak."

"Why?"

"He may or may not be gorgeously Australian." Amy gasps.

"HOW— WHA— Okay, I'm moving to Oahu."

"You'd like his older brother. Daniel Hensley. He's twenty."

"What does he look like?"

"Dark brown hair and tall, but not as tall as Sawyer."

"How tall is Sawyer?"

"Six foot two? Six foot three? Somewhere around there."

"Woah."

"Yep."

"You are introducing us during winter break. Have you heard the new All Time Low album?"

"Yes. It is amazing. A-MA-ZING."

"Totally. I've gotta go, my mom's calling me to lunch. Later, Surfer Girl."

"Later, City Chick."

TWENTY

"Are you ready?" I inquire.

"Just open the door for crying out loud! These are heavy!" Sawyer exclaims. McKayla groans in agreement. I laugh and turn the knob of my front door, which is only five minutes away from the Hensleys' house and Grammy and Papaw's house.

My mom found a place right smack dab in the middle of the two houses that couldn't be more perfect for me and bought it almost upon arrival. Today is moving day. I've been accumulating furniture for over a week, and I think I might be the leading expert on buying couches and shelves now. The postal service has been busy this week with boxes upon boxes of my stuff from both of my parents' houses, all of which is now in my grandparents' beater and my "new" used car. I ended up not leaving at all, but Amy is coming for a few days of Christmas break so we can hang out. My mom filled out all the paperwork and notified everyone, so I'm now an official North Shore High School senior, as well. The first two weeks of school have gone fairly well.

Regionals were a few days after my birthday, and, with Sally and I out of the game, McKayla placed second to Paige LeGroe in the girls' under eighteen and Sawyer placed first in the boys' under eighteen, since registration closed before he turned eighteen. In fact, he did so well, a few sponsors approached him about his pro surfing career. Suffice it to say, he can't wait until January.

As we enter the house, the entryway is well-lit by the big window to the left of the door, spilling sunlight over the entire open-area kitchen and living room. The walls are a very light tan and give everything a natural, cozy sort of feeling. In the living room to the left is a big leather sectional not unlike the one at my grandparents' house and a glass-top coffee table with black metal legs. The entertainment center around the TV is white wood with glass panes over the doors to showcase the photos or DVDs displayed there.

On the right is the kitchen and dining room. The cabinets are white, but the countertops are dark granite and an island of the same color scheme is positioned in the center of the room. All the appliances are stainless steel, which gives it a very polished, clean look. The dining room is set up next to another window opposite the kitchen, with one side of the table's chairs being replaced by a window seat underneath the glass panes, while the other side has a bench, and a chair sits at each end.

I set the box in my arms down at the beginning of the hallway, which the entryway to is between the kitchen and living room. Sawyer and Mac set their boxes on top of mine and follow me back out to the car. Once we've piled up a fairly sizable amount of parcels, I begin unpacking and they keep unloading.

After my new dishes are unloaded and the living room and kitchen are put away for the most part, I start dragging boxes into my bedroom and the guest room beside it and unpacking them. My bedroom is very similar to the one I had at Grammy and Papaw's, yet it feels more like an adult's bedroom as I unload the boxes.

The bedcovers still display the poster for *The Endless Summer*, although my posters have moved to the basement, along with both of my guitars. The walls are my favorite shade of teal, almost identical to the board Sawyer gave me, which is now propped up against the wall in the corner. Julia's artwork is displayed not only on the board, but around several rooms of my house. A painting of roses practically interchangeable with the ones on the board hangs beside a few photo frames in the living room on the wall to the left from the entry. Sawyer hangs on the door frame and glances around the room. "Looks good," he states. "Are you done? Because we've got a few things we need your help with outside."

"Yeah, I've just got one more box and it's for the bathroom," I reply, standing and toting said box across the hall. The bathroom is a coral pink, with a white sink, toilet and bathtub, and it's small enough that it only takes me a few minutes to get my stuff put away. "Done," I state, picking up the box and throwing it in the trash. He smiles deviously and I raise an eyebrow at him.

I follow him back out, but this time, he leads me past my car to his dad's car, a silver Chevy that Sawyer doesn't usually drive. McKayla leans up against the side of the car, waiting for us. "Okay, what's the one thing you told me you wanted and your new house wouldn't be complete without?"

"Uh," I say, unsure. "Your sister's artwork?"

"Nope," he rejects.

"A movie theater?"

"Nuh-uh."

"The original Starry Night painting by Van Gogh?"

"Not even close."

"I'm lost here, Sawyer," I give up.

"Alright, open the door, Mac," Sawyer instructs. She does so and he reaches in for something I can't see, but I can hear. Something gives a little tiny "yip!" and I gasp as Sawyer straightens up again, holding a little brown, white and black Cavalier King Charles Spaniel in his arms. "Oh my gosh!" I exclaim, my hand automatically clapping over my mouth.

"She's a little girl, only seven weeks old," Sawyer informs. "And she doesn't have name yet."

"Where did you find her?" I ask, petting her silky fur.

"A friend of mine works at the pet shelter over on the other side of the island and Julia wanted to get a cat," he explains. "So we were already planning to go that day you told us you were staying. That's why I called you to ask what kind of dog you'd want. When I saw her, I knew she had to be yours."

"She's mine?" I repeat incredulously.

"She's yours," he answers, smiling.

"She's perfect," I state happily. "Thank you!"

"You're welcome," he laughs, handing her to me. "So, any name ideas?"

"Not a clue." I pet the squirmy little ball of fuzz and she licks my chin, making me laugh.

"What about Jane?" Mac suggests. "After one of your favorite authors, Jane Austen, and one of your favorite characters, Jane Thompson, from *Three Hours Too Soon.*"

"Jane," I echo. "I like it."

"Jane it is, then," Sawyer agrees.

"Thank you," I repeat to Sawyer, planting a small kiss on his cheek.

"You're welcome," he answers. I set Jane down on the grass and hold tightly to her leash as she excitedly sniffs the dirt. She looks back at me with her big brown eyes and starts running around my feet.
It turns out that Sawyer got everything she'd need already, so he starts carrying in her crate and some toys, while McKayla and I take her around the back to the yard, which, thankfully, is already fenced in.

"Jane!" I call, getting down in the dirt to play with her. "Come here, Jane!" She looks at me for second, then runs up to my lap as I pat the ground.

"She's all settled," Sawyer announces a minute later, appearing from inside. "Her kennel is in the basement."

"Perfect," I say. I ruffle Jane's floppy ears and scratch her head.

"I need to get moving on dinner."

"Fajitas!" Sawyer exclaims in a somewhat Mexican accent. I laugh. "To the kitchen!"

Sawyer and Mac take turns helping with dinner and playing with Jane, which sort of qualifies as helping with dinner, because it's not exactly easy to cook fajitas with an energetic puppy prancing around your heels. Around 5:30, the doorbell rings and Jane races to greet Grammy. "Aw!" she exclaims, seeing the surprise addition to the household.

"Grammy, meet Jane," I introduce. "Sawyer got her for me."

"She is adorable!" Grammy gushes, scratching Jane's ears.

"Where's Papaw?" I inquire curiously.

"He had to run an errand before he could come," she replies with a mischievous twinkle in her eye. Before I can question her further, the doorbell rings again and the Hensleys enter.

"Hey little one!" Julia cries, dropping to her knees to pet Jane. "She's gotten so big! What'd you decide to name her?"

"Jane," I reply.

"Cute," she compliments, nodding.

"Oh, Andrea," Melissa sighs. "Your house is so cute! It's very you."

"Thanks. I like it," I reply. I wink at her and she smiles.

"These pictures are good. Who took them?" Daniel inquires, gesturing to the photos hanging on the living room wall.

"Most of them, my friend Amy took. The polaroids are mine, though." I cross to the wall and glance around, looking for a photo of Amy. "That's Amy," I point out, indicating her image in a snapshot of the two of us.

"Cool," he comments. The doorbell rings yet again and this time, it's Papaw, carrying a familiar bright pink suitcase under one arm. I say familiar, because that same suitcase has sat in my bedroom in New York for countless sleepovers and weekends together. Behind him trails the very girl I have just shown Daniel.

"Amy!" I cry, dashing to hug her. "What are you doing here?!"

"I couldn't wait until winter break," she says. "So I just decided to come!"

"You are crazy," I laugh. "Everybody, this is Amy, my friend from New York. Amy, that's Sawyer," I introduce, pointing each person out. "This is McKayla. You two have met before. You've also met my Grammy and Papaw. Then, this is Sawyer's sister, Julia, his mom Melissa, his dad Eric, and his older brother Daniel." I give her a wink as I introduce Daniel, who seems to have gone mute since Amy walked in the door. Amy's mouth falls open ever so slightly.

"Oh, sorry," Daniel says, shaking his head a bit and holding out his hand. "Hi. It's nice to meet you."

"Nice to meet you too," Amy replies. Jane starts running around their feet and barking, breaking their trance. "Aw! Who's this one?"

"That is Jane, my puppy Sawyer got me," I inform. "Who's ready to eat?"

"Let's go!" replies Sawyer. We all gather in a circle and join hands to pray. Papaw says grace.

"Heavenly Father, we thank you for Annie and here new home here. We pray your blessing on her home and her relationships, and the same for the rest of us here. We thank you for this food and for the hands that prepared it. In Jesus name we pray, amen."

As we unlink our hands, I can't help but notice that Daniel is a little hesitant to let go of Amy's hand. "They look friendly," Sawyer comments softly to me. I follow him through the line and dish up my fajitas.

"Well, meeting like normal people probably helps a relationship. You know, as opposed to getting kicked in the eye," I reply.

He dramatically mimes stabbing himself in the heart, sticking his tongue out to fake his death. "That hurt."

"You know I'm kidding," I say, kissing his cheek and taking a seat next to him on the couch.

"I really never thought I would see you do that," Amy comments.

"Ditto," Mac agrees.

"What can I say?" I reply. "I found my exception."

"Exception to what?" Daniel inquires.

"The exception to my promise that I'd never fall in love," I explain. "I swore I'd never fall in love, because it didn't exist. He showed me it does, and I made an exception and fell in love with him."

"That is the cutest thing ever," Amy states. Jane barks, reminding us that she is actually the cutest thing ever, and noses my fingers. I pet her small body and continue eating and chatting with the others.

Later, Amy gets settled in the guest room and everyone but she and McKayla go home. I pop the disc for *Pride and Prejudice* in the player and camp out on the couch. Jane curls up on my lap and falls asleep almost immediately. "You never stop watching this movie, do you?" Mac says.

"It is a truth universally acknowledged that a young woman in possession of a love of literature can never have enough *Pride and Prejudice*," I retort.

"Good point," she laughs, collapsing onto the other side of the couch.

"So, Amy, was I right or was I right?" I question.

"You were right," she admits, unable to suppress a grin.

"I'm lost," Mac interrupts. "What are we talking about?"

"I told Amy she would like Daniel," I fill her in.

"Ohhhh," she replies understandingly.

"I can't believe you live here," Amy says, looking around.

"I don't either, yet," I reply, doing the same.

"Well, you've got plenty of time to adjust," Mac laughs. As we watch the movie, I think about what I said to McKayla a few weeks ago about being wrong about Sawyer and love.

So, maybe I was wrong. Most people hate admitting they were wrong. In my case, though, being wrong means that I don't have to look to stories and music to distract me from life and feel like someone who is loved. It means I am loved, not just by Sawyer, but by my mother and father and all of my friends and family. It means I've recognized what was already there for the most part and have accepted what wasn't there. My life is, in fact, a hundred times better than any girl just getting swept off her feet by a handsome stranger. You think getting swept off your feet is crazy? Try getting kicked in the face. It's much more interesting. All I know is my life is finally good enough to me.

I'm glad I was wrong.

TWENTY-ONE

"Andrea! How's your knee?"

"Miss Maverick! How have you prepared for your first ASP competition?"

"How do you respond to making it to the semi-finals?"

"Is it true you're dating Sawyer Hensley?"

"I can answer that last one," Sawyer comments off to the side to me. I giggle as he presses his lips to mine.

"Alright lovebirds," McKayla interrupts and we pull apart. "You're not here to kiss. You're here to surf!"

"Heck yeah we are!" Sawyer exclaims, charging for our roped off area. The rest of us follow, "us" being McKayla, Grammy, Papaw, Melissa, Julia, Daniel, Eric and Amy, who is here as part of her Christmas break and a few days after. Oh, and Jane, who is currently entangling Amy's legs in her leash and yipping at all the excitement around her.

"Ladies and gentlemen, welcome to the 28th Annual Pro Curl!" a commentator announces over the sound system. I tune out the rest of his announcements as I pull on my rash guard (White, number 47) and wax my board. Yep. I'm really at the Pro Curl. And I'm really competing.

Actually, Sawyer and I both made the cut. McKayla decided not to, even though she's good enough to at least make the competition, because she's not eighteen yet and she's planning on going to college next fall and giving up competitive surfing, so she doesn't want to start a pro career now. My qualifying heat was two days ago and his was the day before that. Yesterday was quarter finals and today is semi finals and, if we make it, finals.

This competition is a little different from the ones earlier this summer in that: 1. Everyone is over eighteen. Some years, seventeen year olds make the cut through an evaluation by the Association of Surfing Professionals, but it's extremely rare. 2. The divisions are by gender only, instead of gender and age. If you're good enough to be here, it doesn't matter how old you are. 3. It's the major leagues.

We're criticized much more ruthlessly, which makes it harder to get a good score, and I'm up against surfers like Carissa Moore, Stephanie Gilmore and Tyler Wright. Carissa is the defending champion of four ASP competitions, and Stephanie and Tyler are each defending champs of one ASP competition. Long story short, I'm a little jittery.

"Hey," Sawyer snaps me out of my thoughts, crossing from behind his board to sit down beside me. "Don't do that."

"Do what?"

"Don't be nervous," he commands. "You placed seventh yesterday. You were fifteenth in the Oahu Junior before you stole the top spot. That's eight places lower than you are right now. You're psyching yourself out."

"How can you tell I'm nervous?" I inquire, amazed he can tell all this without me saying anything.

"You were extremely concentrated for simply waxing your board," he explains. "When you're nervous, you either smack talk and get really defensive, or you get really intense about everything." He weaves his fingers tightly with mine. "You're going to be fantastic. Don't just sit here and worry. Enjoy it! You're at the Pro Curl!" I laugh, and he playfully shoves my shoulder. I shove him back a little harder and then he knocks me over, jumping up and dashing away from me. I chase after him, not caring that we probably look really childish right now compared to everyone who's getting their game faces on. He runs around behind me and picks me up, swinging me around.

"Andrea! Come here!" Grammy calls, holding my iPad. Sawyer sets me down and my stomach aches from laughing. I run over towards her and wave at my dad on the screen from over Grammy's shoulder.

"Hey! There's my surfer girl!" he exclaims.

"Hey Dad!" I greet. "Are you at the office?"

"Yes, I am. And you know what's playing in the lounges right now?" he chides.

"What?"

"A certain surf competition that you might be watching too," he replies. "Check it out!" He turns the camera around and shows me a cluster of employees gathered in the break lounge of the top floor of his office building, watching the Pro Curl coverage.

"Sweet!" I laugh.

"Good luck kiddo!" he wishes. "When you're on, we'll be cheering for you!"

"Thanks Daddy!" I respond. "I love you!"

"I love you too! Call me when it's over!" He hits the "end call" button and almost immediately, they call my heat for semi-finals.

"Remember what we've been working on," Papaw coaches. "Don't go for the lien alley-oop unless you really need to or you really feel comfortable. Slob airs, stalefish in combos and alley-oops mostly, and make sure to keep your style clean." I nod.

As soon as I found out I was staying, Papaw and I really upped our game with training and I started working out to build up my legs again after my knee surgery. For about four months now, I've been perfecting my hardest moves and practicing the Lien alley-oop, an extremely tough and high-scoring aerial during which a surfer gets four or five feet off the wave and performs a 360° rotation alley-oop while holding her heel-side rail with her left hand. For an alley-oop, a surfer turns and launches off the lip of the wave with the board pointing slightly back and then rotate around to point forward while in the air, landing right on the top of the lip.

The heat begins and three other surfers and I paddle out. I clear my mind of all thoughts of Carissa Moore and all the other pro surfers I'm up against and pretend I'm still just battling it out with Sally Emerson and McKayla. A few waves roll by and I get ready to make the drop on the next one, a monstrous hill of water that's going to break perfectly. Just as it starts to foam a little bit at the top, I pop up and make a clean bottom turn to get me in good position for a 360° carve, followed up by a layback. The wave curls over perfectly for an nice little barrel ride, then I kick out.

As I sit up on my board back in the lineup, I hear the commotion on the shore. I ignore them, and get ready for my next wave that comes about a minute later. This one is big enough that I build up some speed and pull an alley-oop, landing back on the perfect spot of the lip and swerving back up to the top for a vertical backhand snap. With a few more carves, I kick out.

I pull out eight more good waves and the horn sounds. As I paddle in, they announce the standings of the heat, but I can't hear. Sawyer, however, heard and runs towards me as I trudge through the shallow waves onto shore. "What?" I call to him, dropping my board and taking off my leash.

He picks me up and swings me around. Setting me down, he grasps my shoulders and shakes me back and forth excitedly. "You won your heat!" he exclaims. "You're first in your heat!" My mouth drops open as I grasp his arms and Mac comes up behind me, wrapping her arms around my shoulders.

"I'm what?" I ask incredulously.

"You're first in your heat and fourth over all," Sawyer informs. "What did I tell you! You're almost guaranteed a spot in finals!"

"Almost guaranteed," I repeat. "Not guaranteed."

"You are only below Carissa, Steph and Tyler," he counters.

"Yeah, and they could guarantee I don't place," I argue.

"Enjoy it. You are fourth at the Pro Curl."

I lay back and relax until the heats are over. Sawyer ends semi-finals in fourth and only one person, a girl named Lacey Meinel scores higher than me, so I finish the round in fifth. Right from there, I start run back towards the water and wait for signal to begin the race.

"Annie!" Sawyer calls, jogging towards me. "Remember: You've got this. You're every bit as good as they are. You just have to show it." He plants a kiss on my cheek. "Good luck. I love you."

"I love you too," I reply, turning around. The horn sounds and the five finalists dash out into the water.

Out in the lineup, I watch as Carissa and Stephanie paddle battle for the first wave. Their rivalry from past competitions seems to be their weakness. They get too focused on beating each other and forget about the rest of the field, which might be good if they're not worried about me. Tyler heads out as soon as they get back, Lacey soon following. I just wait, and it pays off. A wave better than any we've seen so far in the final builds up behind me and I get in prime position, popping and snapping the lip immediately. I do a 360° carve, then a 360° shove-it to show off my control of the board, finishing with a layback. I kick out to cheers on the beach.

A few more good waves come my way and I pull similar combos, but even without knowing the scores, I know there is no way that waves like this are going to get me first. Not over this crowd of competition. I pull another wave and throw in a Stalefish air, and another with a slob air reverse.

This still isn't going to get me a professional surfing competition win. Just as I start to go for another wave, I remember what Sawyer told me. *"You're every bit as good as they are. You just have to show it."* Suddenly, I know what I have to do.

A stellar wave rolls in and as I pop up, it starts to feather a little bit. Whether being confident or stupid, I make a quick bottom turn and launch a good five, maybe even six feet off the wave, grabbing the rail with precise timing and whipping my tail perfectly into a full 360° lien alley-oop. As I glide back onto the surface of the wave, I shout with excitement and clidro a bit, going up for a vertical backhand snap, a layback and a 360° shove-it just for fun. One final slash sends up a wall of sea spray behind me and I kick out, unable to wipe the grin off my face as I let myself fall backwards off my board.

Pulling a perfect Lien alley-oop has sparked something in me. If I can do one, I can do two, right? I only have two waves left, and I decide to make them count. In the final two minutes of the competition, I pull not one, but two more waves with perfectly executed Lien alley-oops.

Before the scores are even announced, my entire entourage engulfs me. Even Jane gets in on it, wrapping my ankles in her leash. "Choka," Papaw compliments. "You did wonderfully."

"Thanks," I reply, turning back to the announcer's booth. Sawyer wraps his arms around my waist and stands behind me while we wait for the scores.

"And we have the results," the announcer states. "In third place, Stephanie Gilmore." A crowd to my left cheers and congratulates Steph, who stands at the front of the pack. "In second place, Carissa Moore." Another crowd cheers, this time on my right and as they cheer, I notice Sawyer's grip get just slightly tighter around my waist. "And finally, the first place winner of the Pro Curl is," the announcer begins, checking the score chart. "Andrea Maverick with a total finals score of 27.5!"

My hand automatically flies up to cover my open mouth in disbelief. I turn around to look at Sawyer. "Did he really just say what I think he said?" I inquire.

"Andrea Maverick, you are officially a Pro Curl champion," he confirms with a proud grin. I just shake my head and laugh as he picks me up and swings me around. Setting me down, his sparkling blue eyes meet mine and he gently grasps my face in his hands. "I told you you could do it," he says, fitting his lips to mine. I smile through the kiss and pull away after a second.

"Now it's your turn," I tell him. He smiles wide and runs for his board.

My success is apparently contagious. Sawyer pulls several brilliant airs and some sick carves and performs well enough to earn himself second place in the mens's division. We talk to a lot of reporters between the score announcement and the award presentation. I walk around in a bit of a daze, before and after my name is called and I get my trophy. Both Carissa and Stephanie congratulate me and I them, then the entourage and I head back to my house.

After starting a campfire in my backyard, we let Jane loose and just stand around talking. As I stare up at the stars, I pose the question "Could this day be more perfect?"

"I can only think of one thing that would make it better," Daniel replies, looking, not at me, but at Amy, who is by his side.

"What's that?" Amy inquires.

Daniel doesn't say anything. Then, all of a sudden, he leans in and kissing her by surprise. I smile at McKayla as her mouth drops open and she glances at me. Amy giggles as she and Daniel pull apart.

"Yep. This day is officially perfect," she agrees.

Sawyer laughs and holds my hand. I lean my head on his shoulder. "I couldn't have said it better myself."

The next day, I wake and check my email, per Papaw's instruction. Apparently, quite a few sponsors wanted to talk to him about me after finals last night.

I scroll through a few unbelievable offers from sponsors (it appears Vitamin Water and Rip Curl like me a lot), then suddenly click the wrong tab on the side on accident. Before I switch back, though, Mr. Clarke's email from a few months ago catches my eye.

"Dear Miss Maverick,

Earlier today, I received my finalized class lists. You seem not to be on any of them. I recall you saying you would be back unless something drastic happened before you left. I expect a five page narrative essay on what happened, so as to have an answer when Miss Carver begins to question me.

Sincerely,

Mr. Clarke."

I ponder this for a moment, then decide the sponsors can wait a little while. I switch to a writing program and let the little black cursor flash at me for a moment as I wonder how to begin. Well, I suppose I should start from the very beginning. It all started the day I left, when Amy told me about her camping trip. *A high pitched shriek pierces the silence of the back hallway of Allerton High.* That's really where it all started.

Late that night, I finally finish the story after going back and forth from my narrative to sponsors, schoolwork, meals and back. Satisfied, I type out a reply to Mr. Clarke.

"Dear Mr. Clarke,

I sincerely apologize for my lack of explanation and the time it took me to respond. I have explained everything to Amy, so I don't believe she will be a problem, however, in case others ask questions, here is the narrative essay you asked for. Sorry, I ran a bit over five pages. It was a 200-page kind of summer.

Yours truly,

Andrea Maverick."

ACKNOWLEDGEMENTS

Yeah, yeah, I know. These are those boring things in the back of the book that nobody reads. I'm still going to write them, because I need to say thank you to the many people who've helped and guided me throughout this process.

First: My amazing, wonderful, fantastic Mom and Dad. Thank you so much for all your help. You've been my editors, consultants and more since that first absolutely awful horse mystery novel when I was nine. For that and so much more you've done for me, thank you.

Next: MY TOTALLY AWESOME SIBLINGS!!! Luke, Will and Katie, thank you for everything. You put a smile on my face when the going got tough and I love you so very much. Thank you.

Thank you to my extended family for the love and support you've shown me from all across the U.S. You are so awesome and I love you all so much!

To Mr. Andy Andrews: I once emailed you a question about what advice you'd have for a young author. You told me, among other advice, to just keep writing. Well, here I am. Three years later, I am not writing a book. I have written a book. Thank you. Believe me, I nearly quit multiple times, but I replayed that episode of your podcast and just kept writing and finally achieved my goal.

Thank you to my incredible friends who've supported me through it all. You guys were my first readers and you have no idea how much it helped to know you'd give me an honest (but kind) opinion on the book. You're the best!

Last but never least, thank you to all the amazing young people who've made me realize that dreams don't have an age limit:

To Alex and Brett Harris: *Do Hard Things* was possibly the most inspirational and driving book I've ever read, let alone one that was written for teenagers. Thank you for giving me the tools I needed to do my own hard things.

To Dan DeLuca, Stephanie Styles, Joshua Burrage, Zachary Sayle, Ben Cook, Demarius Copes, Julian DeGuzman, Nico DeJesus, Sky Flaherty, Jon Hacker, Jeff Heimbrock, Michael Ryan, Jordan Samuels, Melissa Steadman Hart, Jack Sippel, Chaz Wolcott and Jacob Kemp (holy cast list, Batman, that's a lot of names!), you guys have inspired me more than you will ever know. To be able to do what you can at your ages is absolutely amazing. Heck, to be able to do that at all is thoroughly impressive. In one night, you reminded me that "dreams come true, yeah they do." Keep up the good work. I can't wait to see where you all go in the future.

Bethany Hamilton, thank you for encouraging my love of surfing and inspiring me. Your determination fueled mine, although writing a book is admittedly much easier than surfing the kind of waves you do, no matter how many arms the surfer has.

Sadie Robertson, some of my friends have tried to convince me that you haven't done anything extraordinary. I just laughed. First of all, modeling with Sheri Hill? Not exactly easy I'm going to guess. Second of all, I know from personal experience that being a christian teenage girl in this day and age is rough. I can't imagine adding "celebrity" onto that and still being as positive a role model as you are.

So thank you. To everyone near and far who has inspired and helped me, thank you. Whether you know it or not, you've changed my life for good. To you, this book is just a story. To me, it's the start of everything I hope to accomplish.

Thank you.

Love,

Abigail